DARE TO LOVE

Back in 1930, when Nellie marries James, the owner of a pottery factory, her future looks wonderful. However, moving into a different social class brings its issues. She is now the mistress of the house, where once she was a lowly maidservant, and, despite being able to help her family financially, they have their own problems in life and she can never resist interfering. But with her strength of character and talents, she will usually win the day . . .

CHRISSIE LOVEDAY

DARE TO LOVE

Complete and Unabridged

LINFORD
Leicester

First published in Great Britain in 2011

First Linford Edition
published 2012

British Library CIP Data

Loveday, Chrissie.
    Dare to love.- -(Linford romance library)
    1. Love stories.
    2. Large type books.
    I. Title II. Series
    823.9'2–dc23

    ISBN 978–1–4448–1146–9

Published by
F. A. Thorpe (Publishing)
Anstey, Leicestershire
Set by Words & Graphics Ltd.
Anstey, Leicestershire
Printed and bound in Great Britain by
T. J. International Ltd., Padstow, Cornwall

This book is printed on acid-free paper

Check out the author's website at:
www.chrissieloveday.com

A New Way Of Living

The Potteries 1930

Nellie stood in the little nursery, her hand resting on her baby bulge. The smock top was now getting tight as she neared her time. It had taken her most of eight months of waiting to get used to the idea of having a special nursery for her baby. But then, she was barely used to any part of the large house or having servants to do the housework.

'You'll have a very different life to mine, Baby. Just like my brothers and sister, I slept in a drawer lined with an old blanket for the first weeks of my life. I never ever had a room to myself.' She sighed and shook her head almost in disbelief. How her life had changed over the past year. Just over a year ago, she had started to work personally for James, the son of William Cobridge, china manufacturer and now, everything had changed beyond her wildest dreams.

The roller coaster had begun when James had seen her potential as a designer of fine bone china. Originally, she had worked as a paintress, but one of the other girls, Florrie, had become jealous of her talent.

She was very friendly with the department manager and conspired with him to get Nellie sacked. After many difficult weeks, trying to help keep her family together, Nellie got a job as a maid in the Cobridge family home. This very same house where she was now mistress.

'And Baby, your dear father gave me paints and paper and a space to work . . . just along here, it was in an old dressing room. He loved my pictures. Your grandma liked some of them too. The fairy plates. I wonder if you will be a little girl and will like my fairy pictures, too? If you're a boy, I shall have to think of something else special, just for you.'

Nellie gave a little laugh. Was it because she was pregnant that she was becoming so maudlin? Reminiscing more and more each day she drew closer to the birth. She continued her tale, almost believing her baby could be listening.

'Then I saw some of the work by the new painters with whole new styles of pottery. Clarice Cliff and Susie Cooper were becoming all the rage. I put my own slant on it and James had the confidence to try it out. Despite his traditionalist father, James did it. And we fell in love on the way. Cost me my job as maid, really, but it didn't matter in the end.' She gave another sigh. It had been a very difficult time but they had come through it.

'And then you asked me to marry you, James,' Nellie whispered to the empty room. 'And I said yes.'

James had broken the news to his parents at dinner one evening. He had recounted to her exactly what they had said, word for word.

'I take it this is some sort of joke?' his mother had said in a cold voice.

'She's the best you can do?' suggested his father. 'If you've got the child into trouble, I'll pay her off. Make sure she's got enough to look after the brat.'

'How dare you. Both of you. Nellie is a wonderful girl. I love her and no, I have not got her into trouble, as you put it. I shall marry her and if you don't like it, then we won't invite you to the wedding.'

'James. How can you bring us down like this? There are dozens of respectable girls who'd give anything to marry you. You have a position to keep up. A status. You're respected in this town, as is your father and all the family. People will talk.'

'Because I'm marrying the girl I love, and a very talented one, at that? Excuse me.' He threw his napkin onto the table and left the room. His parents continued to debate the horrors of the situation as they saw it, long after the meal was finished.

'I shall disinherit him if he goes ahead,' Mr Cobridge said.

'But you can't. How will you manage without him? He's practically running the factory since you've been unwell.'

'We've got managers in the various departments. I'll soon pick up the reins again.'

'And these new lines he says are so popular. Who will organise them? Not that I like them myself. Very crude.'

'Don't worry. The girl will soon drop him once she knows he'll be cut off without a penny.'

'I'm not so sure of that. But we shall see.'

All credit to him, James had stuck to his guns, ignoring his father's threat. Few people had believed they would actually get married and the opposition was such that it had all happened in great secrecy. They told no-one at the time and even had to remain apart, staying in their own homes for a time. Once the news had broken, the newly weds had been forced to leave the factory, find somewhere to stay and new jobs.

'I'm so sorry, Nellie,' James had told her. 'This wasn't what life was supposed to be like.'

'I'd have loved you rich or poor,' she assured him. As things turned out, she had coped much better than he had. She was used to the grinding poverty of life through the General Strike and the difficult times of life in a mining family. The poverty hit him hard. He had never known what it was like to do without anything.

'And was it then his father died?' Nellie asked her baby (or was it herself?). 'Yes, I think it must have been then. Oh dear, my brain is all over the place these days. His father, your grandfather, Baby, he died and Mrs Cobridge insisted James came to live back here at Cobridge House. He wouldn't come without me, of course. It was a very difficult time then. Mrs Cobridge used to say she couldn't sit at the same dinner table as one of her maids. I didn't like it much, either.

'Then she took to staying in her own room all the time. And eventually, she died there, all alone. Bit sad, really. All these people in her house and nobody with her when she passed on. She didn't even know you were on the way. So Baby, there's me having to boss around the people who used to boss me. Don't think Ethel's ever forgiven me. As for Mrs Wilkinson . . . the Dragon Lady, they used to call her . . . she still tells me how things need to be done. Not that I mind. Leaves me free to get on with my work.'

She gave a rueful laugh. 'Not that I can get near enough my bench to do anything much, cos you're in the way.' She stroked the bump once more and felt the all too frequent tears beginning to push forward.

'Oh, there you are, Mrs Nellie,' came a voice from along the corridor.

'Mrs Wilkinson. You startled me.' She wiped her eyes quickly.

'Sorry, Ma'am. I heard someone

talking and wasn't sure who was up here. I wondered if you were ready for tea?'

'Thank you. I'll come down right away. But actually, could I have some milk? I find tea makes me feel a little queasy these days.'

'Milk? Very well, Ma'am. I'll get Ethel to serve it in the drawing room.'

'Thank you.' Nellie closed her eyes. She'd much rather have sat in the kitchen for a bit of a gossip but it simply wasn't done. With James away at work and not many real friends of her own, she often felt lonely. She had always been used to the bustle of working with other people, especially over this past year.

Her new, bold designs had taken off and made a great deal of money for the company. Many of the girls at the factory had disliked the new lines as being too modern but had ceased to complain when their jobs were more secure and wages were increased.

'I know James doesn't want me to,

but I think I really must go into the factory soon. I miss them all, Vera especially.'

She heard a bell ring downstairs and went down quickly, knowing how unpopular she would be if she kept the maid waiting for her. She remembered all too well what it was like when the family didn't obey the unspoken rules, especially regarding meals. The drawing room door was open. As always, she got a thrill of pleasure, seeing the elegant room and beautiful fresh flowers, all there for her.

'Thank you, Ethel.'

'Mrs W says as how you wanted milk. I've warmed it for you. Didn't think as anyone would want to drink cold milk. Nasty stuff. And there's toasted muffins in the dish. Cook says she's got them special, like. She thinks you need building up but I says to her, you're naturally skinny and it's just the big bulge in front makes you look a bit odd.'

'Well, thank you for all of that, Ethel.

You can go now. I can still just about manage to pour my own drink. Thank Cook for the muffins.'

Ethel gave her a glare as she left. Nellie knew exactly what the girl, or woman as she had become, was thinking. They were the same age and Ethel's prospects were non-existent. She might aspire to become a house-keeper but she had neither expertise nor the talent to learn the job at present. But she couldn't find it in her heart to sack her, despite the frequent moans about the work being too much for her to manage on her own.

Nellie knew exactly how much work the job entailed, and the relatively quiet lives that she and James enjoyed did not merit taking on another girl. Ethel would have to put up or shut up, as her dad would have said. She sipped the milk and wished they had a dog so she could feed it the wretched muffins.

She munched her way through half of one and threw the other half on the fire, hoping it would disappear before anyone came into the room. There were three of them in the dish and she couldn't even finish one. What she would have given for even one muffin when she was a child. They'd always been hungry and the boys and her father had always had the lions' share. The inequality of life still hit her hard, but James was a good man and did as much as he could to make life better for his workers. She heard the front door open and went to see who was there.

'James! How lovely. You're home early.'

'I couldn't wait to see my adorable little wife and her bump. How are you, my darling?'

'Fine. Bored. Fat. Pleased to see you.'

'I'm sorry you're bored, but you look wonderful to me. The very picture of maternal beauty. Now, am I in time for tea? I'm starving.'

'That's good. You can eat up my muffins. Cook says she got them special, like, according to Ethel. Thinks I need fattening up. I'm managing that quite well without extra muffins, thank you very much.' His arm round her shoulders, James led her back into the drawing room.

'Where's the tea?'

'Oh, I'll have to ring for some. I forgot, I had milk. Better for the baby and I'm a bit off tea at the moment. Makes me feel a bit queasy. James, I'd really like to go into work tomorrow. I want to see how everything is getting on. Besides, I'm really bored with just sitting around all day.'

'I'm not sure it's a good idea. The fumes in the factory aren't good for the baby, for one thing. I don't want you getting stressed by discovering things are not being done exactly how you want them.'

'What isn't working properly?' she snapped angrily. 'What haven't you been telling me?'

'Nothing, my love. Stop worrying. Everything is working beautifully. Vera's doing a splendid job in the decorating shop.'

'You're quite sure?'

'Of course. She's a good woman and the girls are working really well under her supervision.'

'When I think how that Albert used to be. Him with his lady friend always draped over his desk. Florrie, she was called. Nasty piece of work.'

Albert was the decorating shop supervisor and had been thoroughly lazy. When Nellie took charge of the new lines, both he and his lady friend were sacked and Vera, Nellie's friend and one-time champion, had taken over his role.

'You soon sorted them out, didn't you? You're a very clever girl, Nellie Cobridge.'

'I know,' she laughed. 'Not that your parents would have agreed with you. It was all a bit sad, really. Your mother was such a lovely lady, right up to the time you decided to marry the parlour maid. Not that I was even a proper parlour maid, really. Daughter of a miner, as well. Whatever was the world coming to? Well, her world anyway.'

'You're far better than most of the stupid girls my mother thought would be suitable marriage material.'

'Only most of them?'

'All of them, of course. Now, are we getting any tea or do I have to make it myself?'

It was pleasant sitting by the fire, chatting about the factory and their plans for the future and the future of their child.

'I think I'm happier now than I have ever been before,' Nellie said suddenly.

'Despite feeling bored?'

'Oh, you know me. Never been one for sitting around. I can't wait to get back into the factory.'

'Yes, well just a quick visit, if you must. But you won't be starting back to work until several weeks after the baby is born. You need time to recover and regain your strength.'

'Oh, piffle. My mother was up and about right away. With our Lizzie, she never took any time out. Didn't have a choice, cos there was Joe and Ben to think of as well. I helped out, of course.'

'How are they all? We haven't seen them for a long time. I'll tell you what, let's invite them all round for tea on Sunday. That should keep you busy. Why don't you go and see them tomorrow and you can ask them?'

'Thank you, James. I think that would be nice.'

'Right. That's settled. I'll come home for lunch and drive you round on my way back to work. I can collect you when I come home again. Your visit to the factory can wait a while longer.'

'I suppose so. But I can walk back from seeing my mum. It'll do me good. I do need to take some exercise, you know.'

'We'll see what the weather's doing. Now, have you thought any more about engaging a nanny? It's only a month to go and you need to be certain you've found the right person.'

'I've told you. I don't want a nanny. I shall look after the Bump myself.'

'Don't be ridiculous, Nellie. You must have a nanny. Besides, you will be needed back at the factory before too long.'

The argument had been running for some time. To James, it was quite incomprehensible that anyone would want to manage without a suitable nanny to look after a child. Sometimes, he found it impossible to convince Nellie to take advantage of a large household staff to make life easier.

It was at times like this that he was aware of the differences in their backgrounds. Perhaps Nan Vale, Nellie's mother, could help him to convince his wife. But on the other hand, maybe she was the wrong person. No doubt that once the baby arrived, his wife would see sense and realise that she simply couldn't manage. Heaven forbid, Ethel or Mrs Wilkinson could never manage. He shuddered at the thought.

'What is it, James? Are you cold? Shall I put some more coal on the fire?'

'Don't be ridiculous. If we need more coal, ring the bell for Ethel to do it. But it isn't that. I was thinking that if you don't get a properly trained nanny, Ethel or the Dragon Lady will have to help out.'

'Oh, James, you are funny. As if I can't manage my own baby. There is only one of him or her. As I said, my mother managed four of us with no help at all.'

'Your mother did not have a position in society. Once you are over the confinement, we shall have to start to entertain again. There are a number of business people I need to invite to dinner. We need to engage another maid too. Ethel is only just managing. We need someone a little more personable to open the door and generally help out.'

'Mrs Wilkinson usually deals with that sort of thing. I'll tell her to look into it. But a nanny? No. I don't want anyone telling me how to bring up my own child.' They would never agree on this point. 'Now, I shall go and dress for dinner, though why we bother with such nonsense I shall never know. Not when there's only just the two of us.'

James sat for a while, staring into the fire. He adored his wife, but there were times when she nearly drove him mad with her ideas. Perhaps he could understand what his mother meant when she had told him not to marry out of his class.

He had no real regrets at all, but he needed to get the household running properly as befitted their position as factory owners in the Potteries.

Nellie was going to make a wonderful mother, of that he had no doubt. She would show affection to her child beyond anything he had ever known himself. He could never remember being cuddled and had only vague memories of his youngest childhood, when he was brought to the drawing room for a short time after tea. He was always on his best behaviour with the two strangers he later learned were really his parents. He'd been sent away to a prep school at seven and boarding school when he reached adolescence.

Being close to his parents was never an option. Nellie had been horrified when he had talked about his young childhood and assured him that no child of hers would ever feel like that. It wasn't as if her own parents had been overly affectionate, but she intended to make up for all of them with their own baby.

Perhaps it was his stories that was causing her reluctance to engage a nanny. She'd said that she didn't want some stiff and starchy woman scaring their child half to death. All the same, it was expected and if she wanted to return to her design work in the factory, a nanny might be the only answer. There was still a month to go before the baby was due, so there was time enough. James went upstairs to dress for dinner. This was a tradition he intended to maintain, whatever Nellie said.

'We Shall Have A Nanny'

'Eh, our Nellie, just look at you,' her mum said the next afternoon. 'Come on in, duck, and let me get a proper look. Sit down now and put your feet up.'

'You've got this room looking really nice, Mum. You are still happy here, aren't you?'

'Course we are. It's all lovely. And the young ones love having rooms to themselves. It was very good of your James to move us up here. I'd never have dreamed we'd live up on the hill like this.'

Since taking over the factory, James had refurbished most of the company's houses, putting in bathrooms and modernising them as much as he could afford. He had insisted that the Vale family should move into one of the larger houses, despite the fact that they didn't work at the factory.

'It's only right,' he had said. 'My wife's family shouldn't have to live in a miner's back-to-back terrace. I won't be charging them the full rent, but you don't need to let them know that. I dare say your dad would see it as charity.'

'You're that posh now, our Nellie. I hope you won't be getting airs and graces above yourself.'

'Course I won't, Mum. I do have to try to speak properly though. I don't want to embarrass James in front of the servants or his business friends. Just imagine, me having servants.'

'I s'pose I'd have cause to complain, but at least you're keeping people in work. We were glad enough of your wages when you worked at the big house. Now you're mistress of it. Who'd have thought it, eh?'

'Yer, you never know before, till after.' Nellie slipped back into her natural accent.

'Good to hear you haven't forgotten everything your dad used to say.'

'So, how are all the family? Little Lizzie will be moving up to the Grammar in September.'

'If she gets in. Ben seems to be managing all right. He wants to take up design. Says he wants to go to college and all that, but I'm not sure it's the right thing for him. Besides, he'll want to be out earning money, knowing him.'

'Plenty of time yet. What is he? Fourteen? Nearly fifteen. Maybe we could take him on and sponsor him through college. That way, he can work part time and study the other days.'

Nan liked that idea and sent up another little prayer of thanks for the great good fortune her daughter had come into. 'And don't fret, if Lizzie doesn't get a scholarship to the Grammar school, I shall pay for her to go. She's a bright little thing and deserves her chance to better herself.'

'Your dad isn't going to like charity. You know what he's like.'

'I can remember he wasn't slow to take up any chance of a bit of extra cash to spend down at the miners' club. I've never forgotten that time I got paid good money for a painting I did. I sold it to raise money for the Band of Hope outing. He spent most of it treating his friends down at the club.'

'Yes, well he's changed now. Since we came up in the world, he only goes to the club on Saturdays. He's even taken up gardening. I can hardly believe it. We've got vegetables growing out the back. You'll have to have a look later. I'll put the kettle on. Dare say you could do with a cuppa.'

The afternoon passed pleasantly enough. Nellie marvelled at the change in her mother. She had put on some weight and looked healthy. No longer the frail woman, constantly ill with chest infections and struggling to hold her family together, Nan was taking a proper role in the community. She still worked for the Band of Hope, raising funds to take the local children on outings and attending meetings to condemn the evils of drinking.

'So, will you all come for your tea on Sunday, do you think?'

'I expect so. It's usually your dad's day for his gardening, but I dare say he'll have had enough by tea time. Besides, you and James always put on a good spread. That fancy cook of yours bakes a lovely fruit cake. And I dare say there'll be some of that nice ham and maybe a pork pie?'

'I should think we can arrange all that, Mum.' Nellie smiled, knowing full well that Nan was choosing all the things her dad liked best. 'And I'm sure James will make sure there's a bottle or two of beer in the cupboard. Do you think Joe will be with you?'

'I reckon so. It's his weekend home from the farm. I must say, I'd never have seen our Joe as a country lad, but he seems to love living out near Barlaston way.'

'Great. I dare say James will run him back in the car after tea. How's he getting on?'

'All right, as far as I know. You know

our Joe. Never says nowt about owt.'

'I s'pose I'd best be getting me sen together. Oops ... myself. James wouldn't like that.'

'He's all right with you, isn't he? Only if you're not happy, you only have to say and you can come back here.'

'Course I'm happy. Why wouldn't I be? I'm only joking. I make James laugh when I talk proper Potteries. He hears it all the time at the factory, of course, but it amuses him to hear me. But as you used to tell me when I was little, *Yew munna say dunna it inna polite*.'

'Oh, get on with you, our Nellie. Look, there's your fella coming for you in his fancy car. See you on Sunday and thanks for coming round. It's been champion. Tek it easy now.'

'Don't have much choice these days. Bye, Mum.'

She walked up the little garden path and noticed there were lots of bright flowers growing in the borders. Such a change from the dreary back yard they'd had as children. It was nice to think her parents had a few comforts in their lives now. She waved at her mum, watching her through the window and smiled to greet her husband waiting in their car.

'Had a nice time, darling?' he asked.

'Really nice, thank you. It was good to spend time with Mum, though I'd like to have seen our Lizzie and Ben. Still, they'll be there on Sunday. Seems our Ben has thoughts on becoming a designer. I suspect he thinks he'll be as lucky as I was. All the same, I wondered about taking him on at the factory? He could go on to college if he's got what it takes.'

'I leave all of that to you. You can manage things however you want to but only if he's got talent. He'll never survive on the factory floor if you show him favouritism.'

'Course I wouldn't. You know me better than that. Now tell me, what are the sales figures like for the new Jazz designs?'

'Not bad at all. We've got several

substantial orders and there's interest in the production of different colours. Same sort of designs, but a change of colour. We need to look at teapots next, though. Nobody wants a tea-set without the option for matching teapots.'

'I'll sketch some out tomorrow. I'd already planned to do them, but Bump got in the way.'

'And how is Bump? Not giving you any troubles?'

'Perfect. I felt quite reassured after talking to my mother. She's given me a few hints . . . which I bet none of your trained nannies know. How could they if they've never been mothers themselves?'

'All the same, I am not yielding to you on this one. We shall have a nanny if I have to engage her myself. It doesn't mean you can't be fully involved in bringing up the baby.'

'Very well, James. But I still intend feeding the child myself. There's a lot written about the benefits of mother's milk to give a good start in life. I shall not be using any of this formula stuff they are talking about.'

James said nothing. He was delighted by this first major victory. He was learning to bide his time and eventually he'd get his wife to accept all his intended changes to their household. He smiled at her.

'You're a stubborn little minx, aren't you? But I love you all the more for it. I shall contact the agency tomorrow and set up some interviews. Would you like to do it alone or shall I sit in with you?'

'I'll think about it. And I suppose I'd better let Mrs Wilkinson interview for an extra maid. There will be a lot more work when Bump arrives. It'll please Ethel anyway. Maybe she'll stop glaring at me every time she sees me.'

'Get rid of her then. If you don't like having her here, sack her.'

'Oh, but I couldn't. There's nothing wrong with her work. She resents the fact that I am now her boss when she was the one who had to train me up to be a good maid.'

'Then she did a spanking good job is all I can say. Oh Nellie, I am so glad you married me.'

'I'm glad I did too.'

Nellie planned to spend the next day at the factory, much to James's annoyance. She wanted to make sure everything was in good order and running smoothly while she was still relatively mobile. Whatever James said about her needing to rest, she had no intention of lazing about for weeks on end. She was in good health and if her mother could do all she did when she had been in such poor health as she had experienced, then surely there could be no problems.

★　★　★

'Mrs Cobridge, Nellie, you're a sight for sore eyes. My, but you're looking well.' Vera had flung her arms round her, remembering in time that Nellie was now the boss.

'Lovely to see you, Vera. How's it

going? I see the girls on the back bench are back on the traditional lines. Are the orders keeping up with them?'

'There's always call for the traditional stuff. Mind you, them big blocks of colour aren't that easy to get even.'

'No, but it isn't vital to get it absolutely flat. Makes it look hand crafted, or so I try to tell everyone. I want to try some other stuff, too. I saw something in a magazine. Colour banding done under the glaze. Bit different, but you can get some nice effects. Anyway, we won't be trying that till after the baby's arrived.'

'Nellie Vale, Cobridge, you're amazing. I still can't get used to you, you know. That little quiet mouse of a girl who crept in one dinner time to pinch my paints and paint a cup. Look at you now. One of the bosses, a married woman and about to give birth to the son and heir to Cobridge's.'

'Might be a girl.'

'Nah. You're carrying too high for a girl. I'm that pleased for you, love.

Excuse me. I need to have a go at Maggie there. She's takin' advantage of me bein' busy. Maggie, you've got two dozen more of them cups to do before you get a tea break. Get to it.' Vera's bellow filled the entire workshop.

'Slave driver. Morning, Mrs Nellie.' Maggie gave a grin. The title of Mrs Nellie had been adopted as showing some respect to her new role. It was a halfway step after knowing her simply as Nellie when she worked there as a girl. Maggie knew well that Vera's bark was always worse than her bite, as long as you didn't worry her to show her teeth too much.

'Morning, Maggie. Morning, ladies. Keep up the good work.' Nellie stepped back into Vera's office. 'Right, well I'm here to finish off some new work so I'd best leave you to it. You're doing really well, Vera. I'm so proud of you.'

'Thanks, love. I feel the same about you. See you later.'

Nellie went into her little office just outside the main workshop. She'd had windows put into it so she see what was going on. She perched on her high stool and pulled her drawing board as close as she could get it.

It wasn't easy to work with her bulge in front of her, but she needed to get her art deco teapot design completed. She had already made preliminary sketches and now needed to refine it ready for the model maker and ultimately the mould maker. It was a long process from conception to production and time was of the essence with her current styles. She needed to get them out there while there was still demand. Modern was only modern as long as fashion allowed it to be.

Once she was satisfied with her sketches for the shape, she took tracing paper and copied the outline. She made another copy and began to trace shapes on the sides for the final designs.

The sharp outline presented a different challenge from the cups as it was so much bigger. Simply enlarging the pattern to match was not an option. It made for blocks of colour that were too large to look good. She frowned and bit on her pencil.

She picked up the second tracing and worked again, using watercolour paints to get an idea of the finished design she wanted. She was still not satisfied and changed the whole shape of the teapot. It was uncomfortable sitting on her stool and she lowered herself down to have a stretch. Seconds later, Vera came rushing in.

'Are you all right, Nellie?'

'Course I am,' she snapped unnecessarily. 'I'm just having a stretch.'

'That's as may be. You've perched at that bench long enough for one day.'

'Has James been getting to you?'

'Well, yes. He ordered me to look out for you. Not to let you work for too long. Oh, I say, is this the new teapot?'

'Yes, but it isn't right. It doesn't quite work. The pattern needs to echo the rest of the set but it's too big. Makes the whole thing look clumsy somehow.'

'You could have two bands of the

main colour at the top and bottom. Just narrow, like.'

'Brilliant. You're right. Then the tall shape of the pot will be brought down and the colour pattern will be a little larger than the rest without looking clumsy. Well done, Vera. We'll make a designer of you yet.'

'Right well, that said, you need to stop working now. You've got the shape you want so that can go the model maker to be getting on with. And you can go home and put your feet up. How long have you got to go now?'

'About four weeks, though I suspect it won't be that long.'

'Well, I'm going to bully you into taking it easy.'

'I will. I just need to finish this design properly and write the notes. Then I promise, I'll go home.'

'Just make sure you do or Mr James'll have my guts for garters.'

Nellie put her finishing touches to the design. She had only been working for a couple of hours but she had to admit, she felt exhausted. It was a good thing she had done most of the work already or she would have needed to work late. She had scarcely begun to make her notes when James arrived.

'Come along now, dear. You've done enough for one day.'

She protested that she needed to finish, but he was insistent. She gave in and with a wave through the window, allowed herself to be bundled into the car and driven home. She had to admit, she was glad she didn't have to walk She was feeling a little strange and the baby was moving violently as if he or she was anxious to escape.

'It can't be coming yet,' she muttered.

'What?' James almost shouted. 'You think it may be time? I'll get you home and we'll send Ethel out for the doctor. It's too early, isn't it?'

'I think so. It's difficult to tell exactly. I haven't got any pains or anything. Just feel a bit odd.'

'All the same, I'm calling for the

doctor. And whatever you say, we're going to get a nanny as soon as we can. She can help you to prepare.'

Nellie didn't have the energy to argue. She wanted to lie down in her comfy bed and have a rest.

She was dozing a little while later, when the doctor arrived. He made his examination and immediately prescribed complete bed rest for the next month.

'See, darling? I said that you were doing too much.' James looked very anxious. Despite having as much money as he needed, there were some things that wealth could not make certain. All the same, he was determined that Nellie should have the best care possible and rushed downstairs to catch the doctor before he left.

'Can you recommend a good nurse? I feel we need someone who can take proper care of my wife. Someone who can actually make sure she gets the rest she needs and who will prepare things for the baby's arrival.'

Two days later, Nurse Harper arrived and the whole tenure of the house began a subtle change. Even Mrs Wilkinson seemed to be answerable to the formal starchiness of Nurse Harper and Ethel was downright terrified of the woman. But James was delighted to see Nellie relaxing and the nursery being turned into the perfect room for the new baby.

It was decided that Nurse Harper should stay on at the house for the first weeks after the birth and take on the nanny duties that James insisted were necessary. Once the child had grown a little, they would employ a younger girl to take charge of the basic needs. It was the compromise that Nellie could accept.

'Why all this fuss, I shall never know,' she complained. 'My mother managed everything herself and had the four of us without any help.'

'And you don't have to, my love. Now just accept that you are not your mother. We can afford whatever help we need.'

'Yes, James,' Nellie said with resignation. 'But they'll be disappointed if we cancel the tea on Sunday.'

'I'll call and explain. We'll make up for it later.'

★ ★ ★

Less than a month later, Nellie gave birth to a healthy baby boy. James was completely besotted with the new arrival and for the first few weeks, came home early each evening to see his son. He was named William Enoch, after each of his two grandfathers.

Life settled into a routine once more and after a while Nellie was anxious to get back to her work at the factory and gave in to the pressure from everyone to leave the baby with the nurse.

She usually worked in the mornings and spent the afternoons at home with William. Her mother often called to see them both at this time, much to the displeasure of Nurse Harper who didn't believe that anything should be allowed to upset her rigid routine. The mother and daughter often giggled as they took

William into the drawing room and shut the door on the nurse.

'Eh, our Nellie, who'd have thought a daughter of mine would employ a proper nurse to look after her little 'un,' her mother said when she called in one afternoon. 'It's a pity our Lizzie isn't a bit older. She'd have loved to look after your little William Enoch.'

'Our Lizzie's a clever little thing. She's going to get a proper education and make something of herself. I want her to have every chance she can.'

'Like you never had, I suppose you mean,' her mother said, a trifle unhappily.

'No, of course not. I got everything I could have wanted in the end, didn't I? But at least she doesn't have to find work and help keep the family together.'

'I know, love. You've always been a wonderful daughter. I doubt I'd have survived without you to help look after us all. I was never well myself in those days. You deserve your good fortune. Well, I suppose I'd best be going home now. Need to get your dad's tea on the table before he beats me to it and gets home first.'

'I dare say Cook's got something left-over if you'd like to take it. Maybe one of her pies? You know how Dad loves them.'

'We can't keep taking your food. Thanks very much, but we don't need it. You've done enough for us, you and James.'

'I'm just delighted to be able to help. After all, it's my designs that have made the factory so profitable this last year. Only right you should benefit.'

'Well, it's good you feel that way. Look after that bonny little lad of yours. And don't take no stick from that nurse. There's some things only a mother knows what's right.'

'Bye, Mum. See you again soon.'

Nellie's mother would never understand the changes her daughter faced. Nor would she understand the fact that she was a working woman with responsibilities and a considerable salary of her own. The next few years would involve social events, entertaining and plenty of hard work.

A Staff Change

It was William's first birthday. Nellie
had decided to hold a party for him the
following Sunday and had invited all
her family and one or two of her closest
friends from the factory. James was
happy enough to show off his son
whom he believed to be very advanced
for his age and always enjoyed having
people filling his home.

He was unaware of the often tense
situation that was growing in the
household. He had always considered
the running of the home to be Nellie's
domain. It was often difficult for her,
when she needed to do a full day's work
at the factory in addition to running the
household and entertaining.

She left work early as often as
possible so she could spend some time

41

with William but he was increasingly left to the care of the nursemaid, a young daughter of one of her 'girls' in the decorating shop at the Cobridge works. Jenny had proved excellent at her job, after having helped bring up five siblings while her mother was at work. She settled in well and found life easier with just one child to look after.

They had also engaged a new maid, Doris, who was younger and much more lively than Ethel. Competition between them was growing daily and the now elderly Mrs Wilkinson was becoming weary with the constant bickering. Even Cook was beginning to tire of the ever increasing load placed on her. Nellie brushed aside the complaints, believing it was just a phase they were going through.

Despite the problems, the birthday tea was a proper feast. As well as ham, salad and pies, there was a magnificent cake with one big candle in the middle. There were trifles and several other kinds of cake. William was showered with presents, many of them hand-made. Nellie's brother, Joe, arrived with a beautifully crafted wooden farmyard and Nan and Enoch had contributed a set of lead animals to put into it. Joe also brought a girlfriend with him, much to everyone's surprise.

'This is Daisy,' he announced shyly. 'She's the daughter of Mr Baines, the farmer, who owns the farm where I'm working.'

'Welcome, Daisy,' Nellie said warmly. 'It's lovely to meet you. Come and meet the rest of the family. I'm afraid we're rather a crowd.'

'Joe's told me all about you so I think I know who you all are. You have a lovely house, Mrs Cobridge.'

'Thank you, but please, call me Nellie. And this is my husband, James. James, come and meet Joe's girlfriend.'

Shyly, the girl held out a hand to shake and almost curtsied as she did so.

'Pleased to meet you, Sir,' she said in a soft voice.

'And what do you do, Daisy?' James

asked, trying to appear friendly, but knowing that he must appear very distant to the girl.

'I'm in the dairy at the farm. Make butter and skim off the cream and everything.'

'We work together quite a bit. I'm taking charge of the dairy herd soon so we'll be working even closer,' Joe announced proudly.

'Beats me what you know about cattle, lad,' Enoch said. 'You're from mining stock, son. Nowt to do with farming.'

'Well, farming life suits me. Mr Bates is pleased with me. Maybe you could come and meet him one day and have a look round the farm. Happen our Nellie could bring you in that fancy car of theirs.'

'I can't drive,' Nellie laughed. 'But maybe James will drive us.'

The look on James's face suggested it would be the last place on earth he'd like to go but he smiled and nodded and left the group to speak to the other guests. Nellie saw Ethel coming into the room and hovering at the edge of the group. The maid raised a hand and beckoned to Nellie.

'What is it?'

'Cook says when are you coming in to tea? Only she's got the ice-cream practically ready and doesn't want it to melt.'

'Ice-cream?' Lizzie said in wonder. 'What's that?'

'Something very special that you'll love. We'll come straight away, Ethel. Ask Jenny to come and take Master William to the nursery. He can come down again when the meal is over.'

'But isn't he going to blow out his candle?' asked Lizzie.

'He can come down again for that. He won't sit still at table, while we enjoy the meal.'

Clearly, Ethel didn't like the idea and scowled as she left the room. Jenny arrived and took charge of the baby while James announced that tea was ready in the dining room.

'Eh, that's quite a spread,' Enoch said, plonking himself down next to the large pork pie. 'And do you have a drop of beer to go with it?' he asked James.

'Of course. And there's sherry wine for the ladies if it's to their taste.'

'I'll have tea, thank you,' Nan said firmly. 'And so will Lizzie and Ben.'

Ethel and Doris busied themselves serving the drinks and everyone was instructed to help themselves to the food. Trying to serve so many different items would have been impossible for the maids and soon they were all tucking in with relish.

The conversation was completely halted and the only sounds were the clatter of cutlery and eating. James had a slight look of disapproval as the company made the most of the spread. Ben and Lizzie kept looking at their sister.

They nudged each other and whispered comments, finding it hard to remember how she had once looked . . . a skinny girl with a pale face and dark rings under her eyes. Now she was a fashionable lady with modern haircut and lovely clothes. She had expensive looking jewellery too, most of it inherited from James's mother.

'You do look pretty, our Nellie,' Lizzie whispered. 'You're a proper lady now, ain't ya?'

'I hope so, Lizzie. And I hope you will be too, one day. We want you to go to the Grammar school when the next term starts.'

'Ooh, I don't know if I'll get a scholarship. And Mum and Dad can't pay for the uniform and everything.'

'James and I are going to pay for it all. And Ben, you'll be doing a design course at the college and come and work at the factory part-time. That way you'll be earning a bit of money while you study.'

'Looks as if you've got everything planned for them, our Nellie.' Enoch was sitting back in his chair, finally having eaten everything he could manage. His face was thunderous and he was clearly angry at the suggestions. 'Have you asked them two what they want? How do you know if they want to go to Grammar schools and design courses?'

'I'd have thought they'd jump at the chance,' Nellie retorted. 'You have to make the most of the talents you've been given. Our Lizzie is a clever girl and needs educating. As for Ben, he's already proved he can draw and he's got some very good ideas.'

'And Joe? Have you got plans for him too?' Enoch demanded.

'Now Enie, don't upset everyone. It's a special day and we don't want you spoiling it by arguing,' Nan told him. Everyone else round the table was beginning to look uncomfortable. James looked as if he wished the floor would open and swallow him up.

'So where's the babby?' Enoch asked. 'It's supposed to be his special day but you've shoved him away somewhere so he doesn't spoil your posh tea.'

'Jenny is going to bring him down now, so he can blow the candle out on his birthday cake.'

'Some stranger bringing up your babby. Doesn't seem right.' He was rewarded with a glare from his daughter.

'I'm sorry if you think I'm making plans for the family, but I only want to do what's best for them. Give them a good start in life. I've been very lucky to have James as my husband. If I can help my brother and sister, then I see it as my duty.'

'And James is in favour of you spending his money, is he?'

'Actually, Dad, it's my money. I earn a good wage at the factory. I'm in charge of the whole decorating and design department.'

'And very good she is too,' put in Vera. 'She's done very well for herself, your girl. You should be proud of her.'

'Well, now. If everyone's finished, we'll get young William Enoch down and he can blow out his candle. See to it will you please, Ethel? Doris, you can clear the empty plates now. And thank Cook for a splendid spread. I'll see her myself later.'

Unable to help herself, Nan began to help clearing and stacking the plates together. Nellie frowned at her mother and indicated that she should leave things alone. Tensions were growing round the table as the baby was brought in.

He had been fast asleep and was grisly at being woken. He had been changed into a smart sailor suit for the occasion and eventually, smiled as he saw the candle flickering on his cake. He waved his hands around and made his own little baby sounds. Everyone relaxed and smiled again and the candle was blown out and the cake handed round.

'Been a lovely party,' Nan said as she hurried the family together.

'Great spread, thank you. And thanks again for inviting us,' Vera said politely.

It took a good half-hour to get everyone into their coats and ready to leave. James drove Joe and Daisy back to the farm and Nellie spent some time with her baby. She even remembered to thank Cook for the excellent meal she had provided.

'Very good of you. The ice-cream was a triumph and the cake quite delicious. Well done everybody.'

Ethel was unsmiling.

'Her family aren't quite up to the mark, are they?' she muttered to Doris. 'Not up to Mr James's standards at all. Don't see why we have to wait on the likes of them.'

'Stop moaning, Ethel,' Doris chided. 'At least we've got jobs whatever you say.'

Soon James arrived back. She put her arms round her husband.

'Thanks, love. For everything.' Nellie was aware that James had found the family en masse to be a bit much. 'I'm really grateful to you for putting up with everyone. I think William enjoyed all the fuss and he's got some lovely presents. Joe's farmyard set is quite beautifully made. I never realised he could do anything like that. And what did you think of Daisy?'

'Nice enough girl, I suppose. She didn't say much though so I don't have much of an idea as to what she's like. Probably suits Joe just fine.'

'I'd like to take him up on the invitation to go and visit the farm. Be nice to see what the family's like.'

'Perhaps you should consider learning to drive. Then you can go where you like. Now, if you'll excuse me, I have a few things I'd like to see to before tomorrow.'

'Do you mean it? About me learning to drive? Oh dear, I'm not sure I could learn though. There's such a lot to think about.'

'Of course you could do it if you really wanted to.'

'Will you give me some lessons?'

'Well, I suppose I could. If I can ever find the time.'

'You are often busy lately. Is there some sort of problem?'

'Not really. I suppose there's more competition around lately. Other factories are producing new, different lines, which mean I have to work harder to sell things that I used to. But, nothing to concern you. I'll finish off the work I need to do and then I can spend time with you and William.'

'But he'll have to go to bed soon. He's very tired after his busy day. Couldn't you finish your work later. I don't suppose either of us will want dinner this evening. Not after that lovely spread.'

'You're probably right. I'm not used to this sort of . . . high tea, I expect you'd call it.'

The young parents played with the child for a while, trying to engage him with the new farmyard. As with all children of this age, he immediately began to chew on the figures. His few new teeth were making dents in the lead figures and Nellie became concerned that he might damage them.

'I don't think he ought to be eating lead anyway. It's something we're trying to remove from some of the processes in the factory. I read an article on the dangers of lead poisoning.'

'But surely they wouldn't make children's toys from something poisonous?' Nellie asked.

'You'd think not, but I really don't want to take the risk. We'd never forgive ourselves if he became sick. Now, I think it's time William went to bed. And I must get on with my work.' He gave Nellie a kiss and cuddled his little boy.

'I'm glad you're spending time with him and that you're not afraid to give him a cuddle. It's so important.'

'I'm remembering what you said. I don't want him to grow up thinking I'm a stranger.'

Nellie sat for a while longer. James was always slightly uncomfortable when all her family came to the house but he was always very polite. He always showed signs of relief when they left. She took the child up to the nursery and despite Jenny's protestations, got him ready for bed herself.

She sang to him, remembering the days she has sung to her little sister.

How the years had flown by. Interesting how time had always moved so slowly when she was a child and waiting for some event to happen. Now she was an adult and a mother in her own right.

A few more weeks and it would be winter again.

At least nowadays, she was warm in her luxurious home. Not like the days she and Lizzie had clung together at night for warmth. William fell asleep, thumb tucked in his mouth. Quietly, she shut the door and went downstairs. Mrs Wilkinson was hovering in the hall and asked for a word.

'Certainly. Let's go into the drawing room. Please sit down,' Nellie invited the housekeeper.

'Thank you, ma'am. I don't like to tell you this, but I'm going to have to leave you. My sister's unwell and wants me to go and live with her to help her out.'

'Oh dear, I'm sorry to hear that. What is your sister's problem?'

'She had a fall and fractured her

thigh bone. She just can't manage on her own.'

'So how long do you think you might need to be away?'

'That's just it, Ma'am. I'd want to leave permanently. I'm getting tired with all the work here. I don't know how we'll manage long term at my sister's. I have a bit of savings put by and my sister's been in service for years so she's put something by for her old age. We'll be fine for a while. She's also been given a cottage on the estate where she worked so at least we'll have a nice little home.'

'I can only wish you well, but you will be a great loss to this household. You've kept everything running smoothly for very many years. I don't know how we'll ever find anyone suitable to replace you.' Nellie was doing her best to remain calm but she was in a total panic inside. How on earth would they manage? The Dragon Lady had been the mainstay of the Cobridge family for ever, it seemed.

'I wondered if you might give Ethel a try? She's been here long enough and she knows pretty well how things should be done.'

'I suppose that's a possibility. We'd have to take on another maid to replace her. Do you really think Ethel could cope? Perhaps if you could spend some time showing her your routine? How soon would you want to leave?'

'As soon as possible, really. My sister is having a lot of problems.'

'Very well. If you can show Ethel as much as you can, we will give her a trial. I'll speak to my husband too. Perhaps he might be willing to give you some retirement payment for all the years you've been of service to the family.'

'That's kind of you. No more than I deserve really, I suppose. I came here when Mr James was still a young boy. Times have changed since the war, of course. And since you were a maid here yourself.'

'Indeed.' Nellie frowned. She didn't like to be reminded of the days when the Dragon Lady used to bully her. 'Yes, indeed. Times have a habit of changing. You can send Ethel to me. I'll see what she has to say for herself.'

When Mrs Wilkinson had left, Nellie clasped her hands together wondering what on earth she should do for the best. She hadn't really considered that Mrs Wilkinson was getting old and wanted to retire. But as for appointing Ethel?

She thought perhaps she should talk it over with James first, but he was very busy and hated to be disturbed when he was working. Besides, he always did say the running of the house was her responsibility. She just wished she knew how to do it properly. All too soon, Ethel was tapping on the door.

'You wanted to see me?' she said brusquely. No deference there, Nellie noticed.

'You have undoubtedly heard that Mrs Wilkinson is wanting to leave us?' Ethel nodded. 'She seemed to think that you might be interested in taking over as housekeeper. I wondered what you thought of the idea.'

'Yes, well I would like to do it. I'd be glad of the extra money and I've seen what she does often enough. Would I get the use of her little sitting room?'

'If it works out, then yes, of course. She does the accounts and keeps the records in there, anyway. Do you think you can keep accurate accounts? It's a big responsibility. We would have to rely on you to manage everything as smoothly as Mrs Wilkinson has done. I'm just not convinced you could manage all of that.'

'You seemed to manage to take over the entire house when Mrs Cobridge passed on. If you can do it, I don't why you might think I couldn't.'

Nellie bit her lip. There might be some difficult times ahead if Ethel was in charge. All the same, she felt she should give her former colleague a chance.

'Very well. You can spend the next day or two learning what you can from

Mrs W and we'll give you a month's trial. Would you agree to that?'

'I suppose so. The job isn't permanent then?'

'It will be, if you manage everything properly, as you'd need to prove you could.'

'And what are the wages?'

'I shall have to discuss that with my husband.'

Ethel opened her mouth as if she was about to say something else. From the look on her face, Nellie knew it wasn't going to be anything she really wanted to hear. Undoubtedly, it would have been some comment about her marrying the boss. The next weeks could be very interesting indeed as well as being rather scary.

Panic Over William

James seemed especially saddened to see the departure of Mrs Wilkinson. For him, it was the end of an era in his life. He had given her a generous retirement gift in respect of her many years working for the family.

'I hope you know what you're doing taking on Ethel in her place. She's never been the most reliable soul,' he had said to Nellie. 'But you've told her it's a trial period, so it will give us time to find someone else if it doesn't suit.'

For the first few days, everything seemed to go smoothly. As usual, the laundry was sent out in large bundles using the soiled sheets as wrappers and came back neatly packed in brown paper parcels. Meals turned up on time and the house looked as clean as ever. Doris was beginning to complain about her workload at times, and Jenny helped out when she was free of her responsibilities for William.

'You seem to be managing well so far,' Nellie said to Ethel when she came home from the factory quite late one evening. 'Is everything working properly?'

'Yes Mrs, but I'm going to need some extra help with the cleaning. There's just too much to do, especially with having young Master William and all his washing hanging around.'

'Very well. You'd better take on someone to help with the cleaning. I'll leave it to you to find someone suitable. I'm rather busy at the factory at present. We've got a large new order and some new designs are needed. We did say we'd take on another maid to help serve at the table and things, but that will have to wait for a while. Right, if there's nothing else, I'll go and see William before his bedtime.'

Some days later, Nellie asked again if Ethel was managing.

'I've taken on a woman to come in

mornings. She needed the work so I managed to get her quite cheap.'

'That's good news. I hope she proves satisfactory.'

'Cook's been grumbling again. Says it's too much for her when we have guests.'

'Oh, dear. There's always something. You and Doris will have to do what you can to help her for now.'

'But that's not my job. Mrs Wilkinson never even showed her face in the kitchen. Well, not when cooking was being done.'

'Well, as we often say, times are changing. Mr James has invited guests to dinner on Saturday. Important business colleagues and their wives. I'll give you the numbers when I have them. Perhaps you can find someone to help on this occasion but I don't want to employ another person permanently, yet.'

'Very well, Mrs.' Nellie frowned. She hated being called just Mrs. Mind you, she had always found Mrs Wilkinson's

Ma'am difficult to cope with. From Ethel, there was the slightest hint of disrespect in her tone. It was as if she would never let Nellie forget that she was once a maid in this house and one lower down the ranks than herself.

'I'll leave the menu to Cook, but if she needs to discuss it with me, tell her to see me.' Ethel gave her a nod as she left the room. Nellie still had a way to go before she earned proper respect from the woman.

The expected company on the Saturday all sounded very daunting to Nellie. Though she was gradually acquiring the necessary social skills, some of James's guests made her feel much more aware of her background than either of them really liked. She was not exactly ashamed of it, but she felt there was something of a stigma attached.

'I'd like you to wear the diamond pendant this evening,' James suggested as they were dressing for the occasion. 'And you must find time to get some new evening gowns made. We have a number of important events coming up and you don't want to leave it to the last minute. I'm proud of my little wife and I want to show her off to the best advantage.'

'But I've got two or three frocks that have still got plenty of wear in them,' she protested.

'That's not the point. You need to dress according to your new station in life. Don't worry about costs and whether they are worn out or not.'

'Very well.' She was searching the drawer of her dressing table. 'That's strange.'

'What is it?'

'I'm sure the diamond pendant was in this drawer. I locked it in here after the last time I wore it.'

'And was the drawer properly locked?'

'Yes, of course it was.'

'Where were the keys left?'

'Well, I hid them in one of my bags in the bottom of the wardrobe. Where I always keep them.'

'Look through the rest of your jewellery cases. Perhaps you put it somewhere different and you forgot.'

'Of course I didn't,' she snapped. 'I'm always extremely careful with your mother's jewels.'

'Your jewels, now,' James corrected.

For the next half-hour, they both frantically opened drawers, cases, boxes and searched every possible and impossible place for the diamond pendant. Nellie was very close to tears as the time approached for the guests to arrive.

'It's no use. Either I did leave it somewhere else or it's been stolen.'

'But how could that be? Who would take it? Surely we can trust everyone who works here?'

'Well I hope so. But I suppose we'll have to ask them all.'

'Before that, you should check on everything else in the house. Make sure there's nothing missing.'

'Whenever am I supposed to find time for that? Besides, I'm still coming to terms with everything there is in the house. I know all the china very well but the rest, well I haven't got to grips with it all. You might notice something missing better than I can.'

'You'd better find another piece of jewellery to wear for tonight. We'll have to deal with this tomorrow.'

The evening was a partial success, in that the guests enjoyed the meal and seemed a lively group. Nellie remained subdued, worrying about her lost necklace. The company included the company's bank manager and a couple of other manufacturers with their wives.

'Economic situation is looking a bit grim,' one of them said. 'You having any problems, Cobridge?'

'Order books are reasonably full at present. Largely thanks to my wife's clever designs,' James said fondly, looking at Nellie. She smiled but still couldn't get from her mind the thought of the interviews with the staff that lay ahead.

'Not always to my taste, this modern

stuff, but it's selling well. Look at Clarice. She's becoming quite a legend, despite all the gossip that goes along with her lifestyle.'

'It's poor Mrs Colley Shorter I feel for. Poor woman. Everyone talking about her husband and his fancy-woman practically living together. Clarice Cliff thinks the popularity of her work entitles her to be totally immoral.' The bank manager's wife clearly loved the gossip, despite her words. The private life of Clarice Cliff was common knowledge and her affair with her boss the talk of the Potteries.

'Sign of the times, I expect,' James suggested. There was the sudden sound of the baby crying. Jenny was in the midst of helping put out the plates and she looked at Nellie.

'Go and see to him.'

'Oh, does your nursery maid always have to help wait at the table?' the woman said with a slight sneer.

'It's a temporary thing. Our housekeeper left us rather suddenly and we've had to have a bit of re-organisation. I haven't had time to take on more staff.'

'Oh, yes, of course, you go out to work, don't you?'

'I manage the decorating and design departments at Cobridge's.'

'My dear, that's amazing. How do you manage to run the household and work away from home? And with a small child as well. Amazing. I simply couldn't do it. It takes me all my time to keep my staff in line. But, I suppose you were never used to that sort of thing until you married James.' Nellie looked away, conscious of the sneer lying behind the words. 'It must have been such a difficult life for you.'

'Not at all. I always had a very loving family to support me,' Nellie said indignantly. How dare this woman sound so superior?

'Now, who's for a glass of port to finish off the meal?' James interrupted. He went to the sideboard to collect the glasses. It had always been his custom to pour the drinks himself rather than leave it to the maids. He stopped and looked around. 'Have you moved the silver tray, Nellie?'

'Of course not. Oh dear,' she murmured and shook her head at James, hoping he wouldn't say any more. This was becoming serious. It seemed an eternity before everyone decided to leave, but by eleven o'clock the last ones left.

'Delightful evening. Thank you so much,' gushed the banker's wife. 'You must come and dine with us very soon.'

Nellie and James decided to wait until they were in their bedroom before having any further discussion.

'That was a rather difficult evening,' James grumbled. 'That Jenny girl was less than capable at serving. Did you see the way she dumped the vegetables on the table?'

'I'm sorry, James. I thought it went quite well, considering the upset we've had lately. It may not have been quite up to Mrs Wilkinson's standards but the food was good. The girls did their best.'

'Well, I think we need to review the

situation. Take on a decent parlour maid and get her trained in the way we need things to be done. Doris had a face like sour grapes all evening and Ethel is a born maid, but not a housekeeper. Anyway, using Jenny to wait at table is clearly a problem if William is likely to need her.'

'I'd like to give Ethel a little while longer. I promised her a month. The trouble is, I'm working so hard at the factory at present, I've had to let the house get on with things by itself.' Nellie bit her lip, feeling James was making unjust criticisms of her. He'd clearly noted the remarks made by the banker's wife.

'Do you think Ethel could be responsible for the losses?'

'No. Well, not personally. I suppose you could say she's in charge of the staff. Whatever else we think of her, she is honest. I certainly wouldn't think Jenny could be responsible either. We've known her family for years. As for Doris, I don't know her all that well but I always felt she was fairly reliable.'

'Well, it's someone in the household. It wouldn't be Cook. She's also been with the family for years. It's a nasty business. We'll need to check everything tomorrow. At least it's Sunday so neither of us will be away from the house. We'll do an inventory, together.'

'Thank you, James. I feel I'm letting you down. I'm just not up to the job of being your wife. That bank manager's wife was positively sneering at me this evening.'

'Nonsense. You're amazing and clever and I love you very much. Now stop worrying and come to bed. Things will look better in the morning. You're to stop worrying.'

'I'll try. Thank you, James. Oh, dear, I forgot to go and look at William. I always look in on him to say goodnight.'

'Don't disturb him now. You need to rest yourself.'

'I suppose so.'

They were awoken early by Jenny, knocking on their door in a state of great agitation.

'Sorry, Mrs Cobridge but you need to come to Master William. He's very poorly and I don't know what to do.'

Nellie quickly donned her dressing gown and almost ran along the corridor to the nursery. William was breathing heavily and sounded very wheezy. His face was red and he seemed extremely hot.

'I should have looked in on him last night,' Nellie moaned. 'It's all my fault. What ever can it be?' She picked up the child from his cot and cuddled him. He was indeed running a high temperature. 'Have you given him anything to drink?'

'No. He pushed it away and seemed to have difficulty swallowing when I tried to make him drink.'

'What do you think it is?'

'I don't know,' replied a tearful Jenny. 'But I think you should get the doctor here quickly.'

'You don't think it could be . . . not diphtheria? Oh no. No, it can't be. Where could he have caught it?'

'I don't know. There has been an outbreak of it in Stoke, but he hasn't been anywhere near anybody. Apart from a walk each day and that's in his pram, of course. We haven't ever taken him out of it when we've been away from home.' Jenny was in tears.

'Come now, you're not to blame. I'll get Mr James to go for the doctor. Keep William warm and try to make him drink something.' She handed him back to the nursemaid and ran to get James. He was already dressing. Nellie described the problem and her dreaded suspicions.

'I'll drive round to the doctor's. I'd send one of the girls, but it will be quicker if I collect him. This settles it. I'm having a telephone put in as soon as possible. It's ridiculous that we haven't got one already.' James was clearly very concerned and ranting a little in his fears.

The telephone had long been a source of dispute between them, but now Nellie could see it would have been a godsend to have it. 'I just hope my uncle is at home. I won't be long.' His uncle was the local doctor who had always served the family well. He was getting old now and planning to retire as soon as he could.

The church bells were ringing as he drove through the quiet streets. Sunday mornings were no longer the formal affairs they had been in his parents' day. He had always hated going to church but wondered now if he should have kept it up. He couldn't bear the thought that his child might have caught what was often a fatal disease. Surely it was poor families who suffered from diphtheria? Not someone with all the advantages they had?

'Uncle Henry. I need you to come and look at William. He's become very ill overnight. We fear it may be diphtheria.' The older man frowned.

'I'll get my medical bag.' They were soon in the car and driving back to Cobridge House. 'I doubt it is diphtheria,' he said. 'That's something the poorer families mainly suffer from and I doubt your William has been exposed to it. Still, I'll see what we think. I was just on my way to church, as it happens. You just caught me.'

'Hmm. He's rather warm,' Henry observed immediately when he examined the child. 'Temperature is raised. His throat looks very sore, poor little chap. We'd best take precautions, just in case. I'm inclined to think it may be a severe case of tonsillitis, but he's clearly unwell. Keep him warm and try to get him to drink some fluids. Not milk, perhaps. Just water will do and you can dissolve some glucose in it for energy.'

'But how do we get rid of it if it is diphtheria?' Nellie asked. 'I mean, little ones die of it don't they?'

'They can do, my dear.' He paused and frowned. 'There is an anti-toxin being developed. It's not been proved yet but we might try it just in case.'

'And if it isn't diphtheria?'

'Well, I don't suppose it will cause any damage. But you know, I really am not sure it is that. I still suspect he has a bad case of tonsillitis. He is breathing reasonably well and his pulse is fast but not much more than one would expect from an infection and high temperature. We'll keep a careful watch over him for the next few days.'

James drove his uncle back home and returned as soon as he could. All plans were put on hold for the next few days. James went into the factory for a while each morning but came home for lunch and stayed with his wife and child for most of the afternoon.

Nellie was looking pale and had lost weight even in the few days since William had become ill. She ate practically nothing and wouldn't leave the child at all. Jenny had become more and more worried that she was going to be blamed for the baby's illness.

She spent more time in the kitchen and helping with the normal work, than she did with William. Nellie was being very protective and very possessive, even sleeping in the little bed in the nursery.

James had made no criticism, knowing how much Nellie herself needed to follow this path. Henry had called each day and was reassuring about William's condition.

'He hasn't got any worse and I really do think his throat is definitely looking better. You might try sponging him with cool water to bring down his temperature.'

'But surely, that could give him pneumonia?' she protested.

'Not at all. Provided the room temperature is kept constant, it will refresh him. I'm not suggesting you take him outside when you do it. I'll give you a linctus that might also help. Now stop worrying yourself. Your little one is recovering and it certainly is no more than tonsillitis.'

'Thank you, Uncle. Thank you very much,' Nellie said somewhat tearfully. The strain she had been under was giving way to tiredness.

'And get some proper rest yourself. Let your nursemaid take over again. You're already looking rather too thin.' Henry liked this little wife of James'. He had disapproved of his brother's rejection of his son when they had married and as for his sister-in-law, he had seen her as the worst sort of snob. 'Stop worrying now and do as I say.'

'I will. If you're sure he's out of danger.' The doctor packed up his bag and picked up his coat. Nellie rang the bell to call someone to show Uncle Henry out and asked for Jenny to return to the nursery.

'It seems we are over the worst,' she announced to a very relieved nursery maid. She passed on Henry's instructions and went to her own bedroom for the first time for several days. She laid on the bed and fallen into a deep sleep. She was finally awoken by James who had taken to coming home for lunch since William's illness.

'I gather all is well with our little son?'

'Almost. He still has a slight temperature but he hasn't got the dreaded diphtheria. I've been so scared.'

'I know my darling. Come on down for lunch now. You need looking after yourself, or you will be getting sick.'

The spirit had lifted in the whole household and relieved smiles were on everyone's faces.

'I hate to mention it after all you've been through but we still have to sort out the problem of the missing items. We have to challenge the staff to see who is responsible.'

'Oh James, with all the trouble and anxiety with William, I have never given it another thought.'

Nellie Feels Unsure

Once lunch was served and they were on their own, James raised the subject of the missing items from the house.

'Have you noticed anything else that isn't in its proper place?' he asked. Nellie shook her head. Taking an inventory had been the last thing on her mind this last few days. 'So, as far as we know, it's just the silver drinks tray and your diamond pendant.'

'I think so. But I've no idea about the rest of the table silver. We weren't any short when we had the dinner party, as far as I know. Mrs Wilkinson would have known.'

'Hopefully, Ethel will know. Surely there are lists of every item somewhere? A proper inventory?' Nellie looked down. That part of household management had always been left to the staff. She simply never had time to be involved with any of it.

'Oh. James. I am such a failure to you. I've never even asked if there is an inventory. I don't organise the staff properly at all. I leave menus to the cook and don't even notice if something goes missing.'

'But you have so many talents elsewhere. Somehow, we need to get the household staff organised so that it runs itself.'

'Your mother always saw to everything personally. I know she did. I was one of the staff, remember. She saw people most days and made sure everything ran properly. I simply can't do that. Not that and be at the factory as well and spend some time with William.'

'So, what do you want to do? We really need your talents at the factory. Come back Dragon Lady. All is forgiven,' he said ruefully. 'I can see why she was such a tyrant. Ethel is simply too easy-going with everyone. I'm sorry but I don't think she's going to work out as housekeeper.'

'Oh dear, how on earth can I sack her?'

'Offer her the old position back with an increase in wages, perhaps. Give her some other responsibility. Oh, I don't know.' James looked cross and Nellie knew he didn't want to have to deal with it. This was woman's work.

'So we still need to find a house-keeper. How do I do that?'

'Place an advertisement in the local paper or if that isn't suitable, you could use a national magazine. I believe there is one designed for such purposes. I'll get my secretary to organise it if you like.'

'Thank you, James. I'm sorry to be so useless.'

'You'll still have to sort out Ethel, though. It will take a while for the advertisement to appear, so no need to rush. I have to get back to work now but we'll tackle the theft problem together in the morning before we go to the factory. I assume you'll be coming into work tomorrow now we know William is recovering?'

'I suppose so,' Nellie agreed.

She spent some time during the afternoon looking into the various cupboards in the drawing room, dining room and hallway. She could not tell if there was anything else missing.

She looked through her jewellery boxes and again, could not think of any more items that were missing. She fingered some of her late mother-in-law's pieces and knew that she would never wear them. It all seemed rather a waste, but there was nothing to be done about it. She might offer one or two things to her mother if James approved, but then, whenever would her mother wear them?

Her life had certainly changed but it had brought with it a whole new range of concerns. Who would have thought that being wealthy could cause so many worries? She had always believed that it was a lack of money that was the cause of every problem there ever was. She looked out of the window in her bedroom. The view stretched out over the Potteries. Great clouds of smoke rose from the bottle ovens that dominated the entire landscape. The huge wheels at the pit heads that worked the lifting cages for the miners were dotted around the town.

In the far distance, she could still see the green fields and trees of the countryside and the canals glinted in the watery sunlight as they wove between factories. From here, it seemed a long way from the Potteries smell she had known all her life. This house was truly a magnificent place to live and not very far from the grime of the factory and the back streets where she used to live.

Just this short distance higher up meant that even the air was cleaner here. She pulled her mind back to the immediate problems. She needed to get the house-keeping sorted and she could concentrate on what she enjoyed doing most.

After breakfast the next day, James and Nellie called Ethel into the breakfast room. She looked nervous and stood twisting her hands together in a manner that Mrs Wilkinson would have come down on like a ton of bricks. James looked at Nellie to speak first. They had decided to postpone the housekeeper problem for a while and concentrate on the thefts that they believed had taken place.

'We have noticed a couple of items have gone missing recently. Are you able to shed any light on the matter?' Nellie said, herself slightly nervous.

'Are you accusing me?' Ethel snapped.

'No, of course not. I, we, wondered if you have noticed anything?'

'The silver tray Mr James serves drinks from off of,' she replied. 'But I thought as how he'd moved it somewhere.'

'Had there been anyone in the house? A stranger, for example? A workman doing any repairs?' James asked.

'No, sir. Nobody.'

'Then we need to see the rest of the staff. Ask them to come in one by one, please.'

'You don't think as how any of them would pinch anything?'

'Nobody is being accused. We're just trying to find out if anyone knows anything. We think some of my wife's jewellery is missing. Does anyone different clean her room?'

'No, sir. I usually do it myself. Till I get another girl took on, I has to fit it into my day.'

'I see. Do you have an inventory of everything in the house? The silver for example?'

'I believe Mrs Wilkinson had a book. But I've never used it.'

'Then I want you to do so immediately. Check through the book against everything and tick things off when you find them,' James ordered. Ethel went rather pale and looked slightly desperately at Nellie.

'What's the matter?' Nellie asked kindly.

'I'm not sure I can manage all of

that. It's too much work on top of everything else.'

'You can read, can't you, girl?' James said crossly.

'Well, yes, course I can. But not long words.'

'Then how on earth are you managing the accounts? She is managing, I presume?' he asked Nellie.

'I thought she was.' Nellie was almost as nervous as Ethel. Truth to be told, she had paid scant attention to the books for the past weeks. One way and another, life was just too hectic for her to pay attention to such matters.

'I think the time has come to review your position here, Ethel. I suspect the housekeeper's job is probably a bit much for you. With my wife's involvement at the factory, we have left you with far too much to do. Too many responsibilities.' Ethel looked as if she was about to burst into tears. 'Perhaps you will send Doris in to see us.'

The woman left the room, shutting the door rather noisily, the instant tears she had shown giving way to her normal, more angry disposition.

'I'm sorry, darling. I felt it was the appropriate time to deal with the housekeeper post. Thought it better coming from me.'

'Instead of feeble little me?' Nellie asked.

'No, that wasn't what I meant at all, I simply . . . ' He was interrupted by a timid knock at the door. Doris came in.

'Ethel says you want to see me?'

The interrogation began again. Doris hadn't noticed anything missing but said she never went into the silver cupboard. Yes, the tray had been missing for a while and no, she never cleaned the mistress's bedroom so didn't know where anything was kept.

With Jenny, it was the same story. She never went into Nellie's room and only helped out when things were really busy as with the dinner party and then while William had been ill and Nellie has taken over the nursery duties.

'Thank you, Jenny. You may go now,'

James told her. 'Apart from Cook, that's it, then. No farther forward. Still, though I believe it's most unlikely, in the interest of fairness we should interview Cook as well.'

It was not a pleasant experience.

'How could you, sir?' she almost shouted when James made his announcement that something was missing. 'How could you think I'd do something to the family wot as looked after me and I've looked after for all these years?'

'Mrs Brownlow, I am not accusing you at all. Not in any way. I'm just trying to find out if anyone has seen anything or anyone different coming into the house. I couldn't leave you out, in fairness to the others.'

'Yes, well things ain't what they used to be.'

'I know. I understand. But that's life.'

'More like that's death. Wasn't like this when the Mistress was 'ere, God rest her soul. Knew where I was in them days. Always got told what was what.'

'Mrs Brownlow, I know things have changed but Mrs Cobridge and I know we can rely on you absolutely. You've always done a splendid job looking after us and we hope that will continue for many years to come.'

'Hmm. Well, I'm not so sure about that. The many years stuff, I mean. But thank you for saying what you did. Now, if that's all, I'll get back to the kitchen. You 'ere for lunch?'

'Not today, thank you. We're both working but look forward to something delicious for dinner.'

'Thank you, Mrs Brownlow,' Nellie added as the cook left them.

'Well, that's that. I do believe those two missing items were insured. They are probably worth more than most things. Whoever took them must have been aware of that.'

'But who on earth can it have been?' Nellie asked. She felt very worried that someone in the house wasn't being truthful. In some ways, she might have suspected Ethel could have done it in revenge for being sacked but at the time they went missing, she hadn't known or suspected her job was in danger.

It was a busy day with several problems to be resolved. Nellie was so busy she gave no more thought to any of the problems back at home. It was only when they were driving home that everything hit her again. Her own deficiencies were quite apparent and had been hinted at by the Cook at her interview.

'What's that old saying? Something about a silk purse and pig's ear.'

'What are you talking about?' James asked.

'Just thinking about me. People envy me for marrying the handsome boss, but they really don't have a clue, do they?'

James stopped the car.

'What are you saying? Don't you love me any more? Is that it?'

'No of course not. I adore you, James. It's just that loving is never easy. Never enough. I'm just not up to the task of being your wife. I can't do it. I can't manage the house. The staff think I'm a jumped-up nobody. Valuable things have gone missing and I never even noticed. I'm useless.'

'Nellie, my darling girl. What are you talking about? I love you and would never have married anyone else. Just because we've hit a few snags, it doesn't mean you are a failure. Look at the difference you've made in the factory. I'd say a very high percentage of our profits are down to your designs over the past three years. Now, I don't want to hear any more of this nonsense.' He started the car again and they drove the rest of the way home in silence.

In the hallway, Doris was hovering. She opened the door and said nervously, 'I thought you should know, Ma'am, I went down the town this afternoon. I went past Blake's, you know, the pawn shop. In the window, there's a tray I'd swear was the same as our tray. The one as 'as gone missin'.'

'Really? Are you sure?' Nellie asked.

'Did it have a price on it?'

'Nah. It were one of them ones with special numbers on. Means it costs too much for most folk.'

'I'll go down there myself,' James decided. 'Explain exactly where this place is, Doris.'

In the kitchen, later, Ethel and Doris giggled together at the thought of Mr James going into a pawn shop. He'd probably never even noticed there was such a shop there before and as for going inside, that would hit him hard. It was an hour later before he arrived back, the tray wrapped in a piece of newspaper.

'Oh, you got it. Well done, James,' Nellie greeted him.

'I'm not sure it was well done, really. I had to pay good money for it. Not what it's worth, of course, but when I told the shopkeeper it was stolen property, he collapsed and settled for the same price he gave for it. I got a description of the person who took it in though. Nobody from this house, thank goodness.'

'Who was it, then?'

'Gave the name of Smith and an address which certainly doesn't exist. Smartish woman. Blonde hair. Reasonably well spoken or putting it on. Late thirties, he thought. Told him she'd been left it by a grateful employer and she needed the money, not a posh silver tray. Fortunately, the pawnbroker had no idea of what it is really worth.'

'One down, one to go. I suppose the pendant wasn't there as well?'

'No. I'll bet she took it to one of the smart jewellers in Hanley. They'd give her far more for it than a pawn shop.'

'Whoever she is, I don't recognise the description. Mind you it could be any one of thousands. Perhaps we'll never know. Let's just hope nothing else goes missing. Now, I'm going to spend some time with William in the nursery. He'll be having his tea now and then I want to bath him myself. Did I tell you, he took his first steps yesterday? Very wobbly but it's progress.'

'That's wonderful. What a clever little

boy. I'll come up to the nursery myself as soon as I can.'

For an hour, the problems faded into the background as the proud parents played with their son.

'You know Nellie, if it wasn't for your influence, our boy would grow up as I did, scarcely knowing his parents at all. You talk about your background and not being able to manage the household but you are a much better parent than mine ever were.' She smiled up at him and touched his hand.

'Thank you James. I do love you and our little boy. Be patient with me and I'm sure I shall be a good wife to you eventually.'

The following day, Ethel asked to see Nellie.

'It's not working out for me here, Nellie,' she announced. 'I can't do with someone the likes of you being my boss.'

'I'm sorry about that. Is it that you really can't manage the housekeeper's job?'

'Mebbe. I'm no good with numbers and writing them long lists of orders and stuff, well, it's just not me. When I said I wanted to try it, I hadn't realised there was so much writing and stuff to do. I thought Mrs W used to have it easy, sitting in her little room all quiet like while we did all the work.'

'I see. So what would you say to having your old job back with an increase in wages? You'd be head parlour maid. And we'll take on a housekeeper and another young girl you could train up.'

'You'd still be boss though, wouldn't you?'

'Well, yes, of course. But I want things to run themselves. I have enough to do at the factory without wanting to manage all of you.'

'I'll think on it.'

Nellie nodded. She suddenly remembered that Ethel had taken on a cleaner.

'By the way, is the cleaning woman still coming in?'

'Just three mornings. She does the

heavy stuff. She's all right. Quite a laugh actually.'

'What's her name?'

'Calls herself Franny Smith, but I somehow don't think that her real name. She always giggles when she says it.'

'Right. I assume you took up references?' Ethel looked away and mumbled something. Nellie pursed her lips. 'Well, doubtless I'll meet her at some point. Think about what I said and I'll advertise for a housekeeper.'

Ethel left with a scowl. Perhaps Nellie would be looking for a whole range of new staff. Smith, she thought suddenly. Franny Smith. Didn't James say that the woman who had pawned the silver tray was called Smith? She must meet this new cleaner as soon as possible.

Three mornings, she came in according to Ethel. She must make sure that she was home for one of them. This woman was the only newcomer into the household and must fall under suspicion.

James was relieved when he heard that Ethel was resigning as housekeeper and immediately he asked his secretary to draft an advertisement for *The Lady* magazine, the publication that had originally yielded Mrs Wilkinson.

Over dinner that evening, they discussed a series of plans to make the necessary changes in their household. The telephone was to be installed as soon as possible to facilitate a number of things, including arranging appointments to interview new staff.

They had discovered there was a new domestic agency in town and once Ethel had decided what to do, Nellie planned visit the owner and organise what staff they needed. It would be much better than any adverts in *The Lady* magazine.

'Just make sure we have adequate cover. I don't want another dinner party like the last one when they struggled to serve it all. If Ethel stays, we still need another maid as well as a proper housekeeper.'

'I said we'd make Ethel head parlour

maid and give her an increase over her old wages. That'll help'

'That sounds like a good idea. Once this is all sorted out, I hope I can leave it all to you. Household staff should be your domain, I feel.'

'I'm sorry, I'm not very good at all this sort of thing.'

'You must stop apologising, Nellie. You are still learning and I know it's a completely different life than you were used to. Naturally I don't want to be bothered with household trivia, but I'd rather have an interesting wife with huge talent than one of these vacuous women who talk of nothing more than a hairdo or what to wear. So, don't worry about the cost. Get whatever help you need to keep the house running smoothly.'

'Thank you, James. I'll do my best. Oh by the way, Ethel took on a cleaner recently. By the name of Smith. I'm wondering if that is the same Smith known to the pawn broker. What do you think?'

'Have you met the woman?'

'She usually comes when I'm at the factory, but I shall make sure I do meet her very soon.'

'She doesn't sound terribly bright if she uses the same name to pawn stolen goods. Certainly worth investigating.'

A Meeting With Joe

All plans were forgotten when the post arrived the next morning. A somewhat badly written envelope arrived, addressed to Nellie. She frowned as she tore it open. A scrappy piece of paper was inside. James looked with interest, but made no comment.

'It's from our Joe,' Nellie announced. 'It seems he's in some sort of trouble. Needs my help.'

'Does he say what sort of trouble?'

'No. You know him. He doesn't write well. Skipped most his schooling whenever he could get away with it, but he's always been a good lad. Hard worker and completely honest. He just says, *I need your help, Nellie. Come over as soon as you can. I'm not even sure where the farm is.*'

'We can drive over later today. Remember, I drove them back after the birthday party so I know the way. I have to go into work for meetings this morning, but we can drive over this afternoon.'

'I wish I'd taken up your offer to teach me to drive then I needn't bother you.'

'Mother used to get one of the factory men to drive her, but he's no longer there. Oh, it's all right. I'll take you. Perhaps you could telephone to let them know we're coming?'

'Oh, James, I don't know. I'm not too keen on trying to phone someone I don't even know. Besides, I don't even know if they have a telephone.'

Scarcely stopping to say more than a quick good morning to their little son, Nellie and James drove to the factory. James went off to his meetings and Nellie tried hard to concentrate on her own work. It was difficult as she was concerned about her brother. He'd never have written to them unless it was something serious. Time crawled by and even Vera came into the office to ask if things were all right.

'Just a family problem,' Nellie answered.

'Sorry to hear that. Let me know if you need any help.'

'Thanks, Vera. I'm not even sure myself what the problem is. Everything all right on the floor?'

'Not bad. Bit of unrest between the benches, but it'll sort out.'

The benches were like small units within the main decorating shop. Each bench had its own team of decorators responsible for painting the different designs. Some of the 'girls' were very skilled at painting complex designs. Such decorative plates that were almost works of art on their own.

Others painted the simple bold art deco designs that were so popular at present and more traditional patterns were partly made using a lithograph or transfer that was printed and applied to china. As an ex paintress herself, Vera was well qualified to oversee all the different work that was carried out. The decorating shop was thought of as the main link in the finishing of all the produce and this was where Nellie had first been employed working on Vera's own bench.

'You're doing a great job, Vera. I'm proud of you.'

'Nothing like the way I feel about you. You're such a great lady now. I still don't recognise the scared little kid that used to make tea and fetch and carry for everyone.'

'I've certainly had to change. I can hardly remember much about those early days except I remember always being hungry and feeling cold. I still can't believe my luck.'

'You deserve it, love. You're talented and that's what's done it for you.'

'But you're talented, too. You're a brilliant paintress as well as being a good organiser.'

'I'm good, but I don't have your creative flair. Any road up, I'd best get back or who knows what that lot will be up to. I hope whatever it is works out for you.'

'Thanks, Vera.' She watched her old friend walk through her domain and smiled as she saw her pick up the odd piece, look at it with an expert eye and shake her head at the young girl. A reject that would need to be re-done.

At last James came into her office and said he was ready to go. It was a half-hour drive and would have been enjoyable except for Nellie's worries about her brother. They stopped at the gate and looked into the yard. It was thick with mud and other unmentionable things and Nellie halted, not wanting to walk through it.

'I suppose we could walk round to the garden and knock at the farmhouse door,' James suggested.

'I don't like to disturb Mrs Baines. Not without her knowing we were coming.'

'I did suggest you phoned.'

'Yes, well, I didn't know the number, did I? Nor if they had one.' James said nothing but she could tell from his look that he wasn't pleased.

'Can I help you?' called a man who had come into the yard.

'Thank you. I'm looking for Joe Vale? I'm Nellie Cobridge, his sister. This is my husband.'

'I see. And why would you be wanting to see him at this time of day?'

'Well, he . . . he wrote to me. Asked me to come over.'

'I see. You'd best go round the other side. My missus is in the kitchen. Save you getting your posh shoes in the muck. And you'd best move that car of yours. Wagon'll be through in a bit.'

'Yes, certainly. Sorry,' muttered James, clearly quite out of his usual territory. He drove it back down the lane a short way and parked at the side, hoping he'd left enough space for whatever sort of wagon that was about to pass.

Nellie was standing by the gate till James reached her and together they went up the path. Mrs Baines was waiting by the door and invited them inside. It was a simple homely kitchen with a range to one side and a large scrubbed pine table in the middle of the room.

'Sit yourselves down. I've got the kettle on so tea won't be long. My husband says you've come about your Joe?'

'Well yes. I'm sorry to come unannounced but when I got his letter, I was worried. It's not like him to write letters. Do you know what's wrong?'

'Reckon so. But you'd best wait for Mr Baines to come in. He'll be taking off his boots and washing his hands. Now, there's some fruit cake to go with the tea. You'll take a slice,' Mrs Baines said as she put it on plates. A statement rather than a question, James and Nellie supposed. As they had both missed lunch, it was received gratefully.

'You're here then,' Mr Baines said as he came into the room wearing just thick socks on his feet. 'Right, well let's get down to business.'

'I hope Joe hasn't done anything wrong? Anything to upset you?' Nellie asked nervously.

'I don't think so. Not as yet. But he's brewing up trouble for his self.'

'What Mr Baines means is that he's not in any trouble, but we're worried about what might happen.'

'Please, tell me what's going on,' Nellie said unable to bear the suspense.

'It's our Daisy.'

'Yes?'

'He's sweet on her. Says he wants to marry her.'

'Oh, I see,' Nellie said with a sigh of relief. 'He brought her over to see us for my son's birthday party. A very sweet girl.'

'Innocent she is. Not been out in the world, if you get my meaning.'

'Well, Joe's hardly been far. He's been working here since he was just a lad.'

'I think what Mr and Mrs Baines are suggesting is that Joe and Daisy are a little young to be thinking of marriage,' James said, as tactfully as he could.

'I don't think they've done anything too wrong but, well, Mr Baines has noticed that they're always together, whispering, like.' Mrs Baines was handing out strong dark tea as she spoke and passed them a jug of thick creamy milk.

'So, what has been said to the young couple?' James asked politely. 'Why is Joe so worried that he's written to his sister asking for help?'

'Told him he'd be out on his ear if he touches our girl.'

'I see. And what does Daisy think about that?'

'Daisy does as she's told. She's got plenty of work in the dairy to keep her mind off evil things.'

Nellie pursed her lips, wondering what on earth she was going to say next. It was a great relief to know that Joe's problems were nothing more than those of most young men of his age.

'Can we see Joe? I'd like to talk to him. In private if possible,' Nellie suggested.

'He'll be in on the wagon when it comes. Shouldn't be long. Right. Well

I've had my say. Gotta get on with my work. Farms don't run themselves.' He stomped out of the kitchen and a little later, they heard the door slam.

'More tea?' Mrs Baines offered. 'And another slice of cake? You have to excuse my husband. He says what he thinks. Your Joe's a good lad and a hard worker. We'd not want to lose him, but you can understand how Daisy's father worries.'

'Thanks. The cake is delicious. We missed out on our lunch by coming here today, so it's very welcome.'

'Oh, my dear. Cake's no substitute for a proper lunch. I'll make you a sandwich. Got fresh bread made and some nice home-cured ham.'

The farmer's wife started slicing the delicious loaf and Nellie's mouth was already watering in anticipation. The conversation was almost nonexistent while they munched on the tasty sandwiches as they waited for Joe to arrive

'What wonderful ham,' Nellie said appreciatively. If Joe ate like this all the time, no wonder he was so happy here.

'All our own produce. Even the wheat that makes the bread. Our Daisy makes the butter.'

'Gosh, I wish we could get such lovely fresh produce.'

'You can buy it in the market. We send everything out on Thursdays.'

'I'll have to get our cook organised,' Nellie said.

'You've a cook? You mean you don't cook for yourselves?' Mrs Baines was horrified.

'Well, yes. I work in the factory. My husband's factory. I'm in charge of designs.'

'I did hear something from your brother. Our Daisy was full of what a posh home you have. You've gone up in the world from being young Nellie Vale, haven't you?'

'I suppose so.' She didn't like this turn of conversation. Fortunately, Joe arrived and knocked at the door.

'Hello, Nellie. James. I didn't think you'd be here so fast.'

'We were worried. Didn't know what was happening to you. What was wrong.'

'I'll leave you to talk,' Mrs Baines offered. 'There's tea in the pot. Help yourself.' She bustled out to another part of the house.

Joe poured himself some tea and cut a slice of cake.

'So, exactly what's been going on?'

'Nothing much. Me and Daisy want to get wed, but it seems her father doesn't like the idea.'

'You're both very young. I expect he's worried that neither of you had much experience of life as yet.'

'And how old were you when you got wed to him?' Joe snapped. 'And me ma and pa. They wasn't much older than me and Daisy. He says he'll chuck me out if I keep on seeing her.'

'Bit difficult not to see her when you live in the same house and work together all the time,' James said with a smile.

'Seems to me you've got to calm things down a bit. Let Daisy's parents see what a good lad you are. Why don't you come home and talk about it next time you're got a day off?' Nellie said.

'Cos I don't want to waste any time when I could be with Daisy. I love her. I want to be with her forever.'

'If that's the way of it and she returns your feelings, than all you have to do is wait for a while. When you've both proved you love each other after a time, her parents must see you're right for each other.' James was trying his best to reason with the lad and hoped his common sense would get through to him.

'Don't see why we have to wait. We know we love each other and don't want nobody else.'

'So how did you think we could help?' Nellie asked.

'Thought as you'd put in a word for me. You being so posh these days and all that. Tell him we want to get wed.'

'You'll have to be patient and let Mr Baines calm down. Get used to the idea of his little girl being grown up. How old is she anyway?'

'Seventeen. Well, nearly eighteen.'

'And is she the only child?'

'I think there was a brother, but they don't talk about him. He either left home or he died. Mrs Baines cries if anyone mentions it so nobody does. Daisy doesn't seem to know much about him as it all happened when she were just little 'un.'

'I suppose that's why he's so very protective of his daughter, then. Promise me you haven't done anything you shouldn't?'

'Course not.'

'So, why did you think I could help you, Joe?'

'Like I said, put in a good word for me. Help me persuade them that we should get married. I love it here and I don't want to be made to leave. And I love that girl, our Nellie. I can't see what good waiting will do.'

'But why should they listen to me?'

'Cos you've done all right for yourself. You ran off and got wed and look where you are now.'

'I'll have to think about it. Maybe we could ask Mr and Mrs Baines over to our place for a meal and give us a chance to discuss it.'

'They'd never come. They never go out anywhere, let alone to eat. Mrs Baines is a great cook and she'd never hold with you not cooking yourself.'

'Let us think what we can do, Joe,' James said calmly. 'If we give it some time, maybe things will get better. We need to go now, Nellie. I'm glad it wasn't something unpleasant that caused us to come over here. Things have a habit of working out, young man.'

They said goodbye to Mrs Baines and thanked her for the food. She smiled but looked uncomfortable.

'I've nothing against your brother, Mrs Cobridge. He's a good lad and a hard worker, but Mr Baines thinks he's much too young to settle down. Our Daisy is even younger so however serious they are, they just have to wait a few years.'

'I think that will be very hard for

them. I can understand. James and I got married when we wanted to without a problem.'

'Yes, well I was married young, as well, and that turned out to be a disaster. I expect your Joe told you about the lad we had.' Tears welled in her eyes, belying the calm voice they were hearing.

'He mentioned something, but said it upset you to talk about it.'

'I was too young to cope with a baby. He was a lovely little lad, but he died when he was only two years old. We've never got over it. I was a lot older when our Daisy arrived and we didn't think we'd ever have any other bairns. She's special to us.'

Nellie and James drove home in silence. It was a new problem they needed to think about.

A Father's Anger

Joe rushed out to the dairy as soon as Nellie and James had left. Daisy was churning the butter, her back aching from the hard work. Her face lit up at the sight of him and she stopped turning the heavy handle for a moment.

'Hello, love. What's you doing here at this time of day?'

'My sister's just been over with her man. You know I wrote to them to ask them to help us?'

'That was quick. So, how did it go?'

Joe was not optimistic and told Daisy what he knew.

'Your dad didn't want to listen and as good as told them you couldn't marry me. But they're going to think on and maybe they can get back to us. Our Nellie is a bit two-faced about it. She and James ran off to get wed and I doubt she was any older than you are.

Well, not much, any road. Actually, I don't remember how old she was at all. But they just got wed when they wanted to and I want the same.'

'Oh Joe, what are we going to do? I love you so much. I shan't ever want anyone else. My dad's getting on a bit as well. He won't want to go on working the farm forever.'

'Maybe that's part of the trouble. He thinks I'm planning to take it off him when he goes. Sees me as one of them gold diggers they talk about.'

He took her hand and kissed her fingers gently. They were red from the cold and roughened by being wet so frequently. Everyone knew that mining was hard dirty work but not many of them realised that farming wasn't all fresh air and healthy country living. With a sigh, she returned to the churn and turned the handle to make the butter. Not too much longer to go till the butter's ready, she hoped.

'I'll get back to the field. The cows will be ready for milking again in half-an-hour. Don't know where time goes.'

'And it all starts again tomorrow at dawn.'

Joe tramped across the muddy yard and out through the gate. He was deep in thought. He'd been surprised to see Nellie and James had come so soon, but it didn't seem as if it had done much good. He wondered if he should try to get another job, but Mr Baines would never give him a reference if he left and it would also mean he couldn't see Daisy.

They'd never let her go out to meet him, even on a Sunday. Besides, he loved it here. He knew all the cows by name and knew their characteristics. He opened the field gate and called to them. Marigold had to lead the herd or else they'd never get to the milking shed in the right order.

Funny things, cows. Clever in their way and quite determined to make things happen in a particular order. They were even quite affectionate at times and often gave him a special moo of recognition as they passed him.

'Come on then, ladies. You know where you're going.'

For the next hour, he worked hard, collecting the milk into the large churns. He filled the jugs for use in the house. Mrs Baines always washed them out and left them ready before each milking time and he took them over once the cows were back in the field.

After that, he had to hose down the milking shed and if there was time, he had to scrape the yard. The cattle stood out in the yard waiting for their turn to be milked. It was hard work, but he didn't mind too much. Anything was better than those dark days when he worked alongside his father down the mines.

He'd been a skinny boy, never having enough to eat. Now, he was rewarded at the end of every day with a hearty meal with fresh vegetables and enough meat and potatoes to satisfy even his appetite. There was always bread and cheese or ham at midday and a good bacon and egg breakfast.

Despite all this, he had remained slim and put that down to hard work. But he had filled out and was very strong and healthy. He wasn't the brightest of souls, largely due to his poor attendance record at school. He had never seen the point of studying and as long as he could read the important things in life, he didn't feel troubled by it.

All the same, if he had been better educated, perhaps Mr Baines would be more kindly disposed towards his courting of his daughter.

In the dairy, Daisy dreamed of a future with Joe. She would love to have a baby like little William, Joe's nephew. She would knit tiny clothes for him and they would sit and dream of the future before a roaring log fire, presumably in her parents' front parlour. But her father had put his foot down.

'You are not getting married and that's final. You're too young to know your own mind.' He turned to Joe and continued. 'And if you don't stop filling her head with nonsense you'll be sent packing with my air gun behind you to help you on your way.'

She shuddered at the memory. Joe had gone pale and looked terrified of this large, angry man.

Since then, she and Joe had been forced to snatch odd moments to talk privately and the rest of the time, make do with private looks that spoke volumes to each other. She knew that her father was quite right when he said she was unworldly. She had scarcely met any other men, but she knew in her heart she wanted nobody else other than her beloved Joe.

There was tension at supper that evening. Mr Baines was in a foul mood. The young couple assumed it was to do with Nellie and James's visit and kept silent, hardly daring to speak about anything at all.

'Pass the salt, please,' Mrs Baines said to Daisy: 'Thanks. Is there something wrong, love?' she ventured to her husband. He glared at her.

'One of the horses has gone lame. I've got a load of ploughing to do this week while the weather holds, but Jacob can't pull the plough on his own.'

'I see. Maybe you can borrow one of Ashton's pair?' Ashton was the farm next to theirs and sometimes, neighbourliness could work to mutual advantage.

'Can't ask them again. I borrowed something earlier in the year. They'll think we're a useless bunch.'

'I'll walk over after supper, if you like,' Joe offered. 'They can only say no and they might even say yes.'

'I'll think on it while we have pudding.'

Daisy smiled at Joe and planned that she would ask her mother to let her go with Joe if her father agreed to the proposal. They ate the rest of the meal in silence. Mr Baines finished his apple pie and custard and sat back.

'You'd better get a move on if you're going,' he announced. His decision was made and Joe's offer taken up. 'Now,

I've got a bit of work to do so I'd appreciate some quiet.'

They cleared the table and took the pots out to the scullery.

'Is it all right if I go with Joe for the walk?' Daisy asked her mother.

'Your dad won't like it. But it's a nice evening. Go on with you. I'll say you're out in the dairy if he asks. Stay out of sight when you get to Ashton's though. Else the old man might say something to give you away.'

'Thanks, Mum. I'll help with the pots later, if you like.'

She ran after Joe and soon caught up with him down the lane. It was a half mile to the Ashton's farm so they would have plenty of time to talk. She slipped her hand into his and they grinned at each other, relishing the chance to be free of supervision for a while.

'It's not that my dad doesn't like you,' she told him. 'He's just worried that we don't know our own minds.'

'And we do, don't we? I know I haven't walked out with anyone else, but what does it matter? Our Nellie never had another boyfriend before she married James and she's happy enough.'

'Well, yes, but that was different, wasn't it? He had everything to offer her.'

'And I don't, I suppose? If we got wed against your pa's wishes, we'd be in terrible trouble. I wouldn't have a job and we'd have nowhere to live.'

'I thought you said that's what happened to Nellie?'

'Well, yes, it was. His parents kicked him out. Our parents would have let them stay only there wasn't any room for them. Not unless they'd all shared our Lizzie's little bed.' They both giggled at the thought. 'But he's clever and so's our Nellie. They easily got other jobs and they had a friend they could stay with.'

'But your Nellie wouldn't see us turned out on the streets. We could stop with them. I could help in the house and you could do the garden or something.'

'So, what are you saying? You want us

to run off together and get wed?'

'I dunno. Maybe I am. Sorry, I'm being too pushy, aren't I? Too fast. I should wait for you to ask me. I read this story once where the girl thought it was wrong that she should always be the one who to wait to be asked to dance or anything and she decided she was just as important as any man. It was called being modern. After all, women can vote now when they're over twenty-one.'

'Don't see why they'd want to, myself. But don't worry, love, I don't think you're being fast. I want to marry you very much. I'm just worried that I couldn't provide for you like I'd want to.

'You'll be eighteen soon so let's just bide our time till then and see what happens. Come on now, nobody can see us. Give a kiss.'

They stood in the shadow of the hedge and gently, innocently kissed for only the second time.

'You're so pretty, Daisy. I'm a lucky chap to have someone like you caring about me.'

'You're a handsome lad, Joe Vale. I bet there's a whole load of girls out there who'd fall for you given half a chance. But I'm not planning to give them a chance of any sort.'

'Daisy Baines, you are quite the modern girl, aren't you? Who ever would believe it when you look such a quiet, innocent little thing?'

'Just cos I'm little and blonde, it doesn't mean I'm a mouse. I am a bit scared of my dad though. He's got a right temper on him sometimes. We'll have to be careful. We mustn't let him know what we're planning. But I do think my mum might be on our side just a little bit. She was the one who let me come with you tonight.'

They walked on, still holding hands and soon reached the next door farm.

'You'd best wait here. Don't want them to see you or they might mention it to your dad when they see him.'

'That's just what Mum said. Good luck.'

Dreamily, Daisy wandered a short

way back down the lane, thinking of their future together. Perhaps in a few weeks they could go off and get themselves married. If they came back to the farm with the job done, her father would have to accept it. If he didn't, well he'd lose one of the best workers he'd ever had and his daughter at the same time. Her mother would have to take over the dairy again and their lives would be very hard. It just had to work out.

Joe returned with a grin on his face.

'No problems. They've just bought another young Shire and want to train it so one of their other pair is available for a couple of days. I'm to go and fetch it tomorrow, after morning milking.'

'And they didn't mind?' Joe shook his head. 'That's good. Might cheer my dad up a bit. We'd best get back now or he'll notice I'm missing and kick off all over again.'

They walked back quickly and Daisy slipped in through the scullery while Joe went in through the back door.

They needn't have worried as Mr Baines was engrossed in some papers and scarcely noticed anything.

'Ashton's Shire is available in the morning. I'll go and ride him over after milking.'

'Right lad. Thanks.' He was barely registering the words so Joe left him and went to see what was happening in the scullery. Mrs Baines was making a pot of tea before bedtime. She grinned at Joe in something that could only be described as a conspiratorial way. Perhaps things would work out after all if she was on their side.

'So, tell me about that sister of yours. And her husband, of course. He is the Cobridge of Cobridge china factory, isn't he?'

'He is. Our Nellie is the chief designer. Worked up from being a paintress. Something went wrong at one time and she got sacked. They were hard times and she did all sort of jobs.

'Me dad was injured down the pit and me mum was poorly so we all had to rely on our Nellie to feed us. She went as a domestic to Cobridge House and James took a shine to her. Discovered she could draw and all that stuff and next thing we knew, she'd wedded him and got an important job at the factory.'

'Quite a story. So now she's the boss of a house where she was a maid?'

'That's right. Posh, she is now. Even talks posh when she remembers. But they're all right, them two. James finds us a bit of a houseful when we all go round there, but he knows it makes Nellie happy.'

'And how did your parents feel about all of that?'

'They've always been pleased. Quite a catch, he was. And he's found them a decent house and looks after them a bit, I think. There's talk of my brother going into the factory and my little sister might even go to the Grammar school. Not bad, eh, for simple mining stock?'

'And you like the open-air life instead

of following any of them. Well, you're a good worker, lad. And we're fond of you, but take heed. Don't upset Mr Baines with any funny ideas cos he can be a right demon if he's angered. I think you know what I mean.'

Joe exchanged a glance with Daisy who was busying herself wiping down the sink.

'We know what's right to do,' he said. 'And you never need worry about Daisy. I'd never do anything to hurt her. I love her, Mrs Baines.'

'Well, you can stop that sort of talk right now. That's just the sort of thing I mean about funny ideas. You're both far too young to be talking about loving and stuff.'

'But, Mum,' Daisy started to speak.

'Don't you say another word. Enough of all this. Now drink your tea and get yourself off to bed. It's an early start tomorrow with the ploughing and all.'

Despite his weariness, Joe lay awake in his little attic room. He was turning over and over in his mind everything that had happened that day. Nellie's visit didn't seem to have achieved anything he'd hoped for. But he knew that Daisy loved him and he loved her.

Not that he was entirely certain what love was. If it was the warm feeling he got in his belly when he was near to her, then he loved her. But as long as he said it to her, it was all she seemed to want. As for being married, it did seem the logical thing to do. Daisy had once said she'd love to have a baby like young William, but he knew they couldn't cope with that side of things, not for a good few years yet.

They snatched odd moments to talk about their future whenever they could but it was always difficult to manage without Mr Baines seeing them.

⋆ ⋆ ⋆

'I've got a surprise for you at supper tonight,' Daisy whispered one afternoon.

'Oh yes, and what might that be?' he said disarming her with his cheeky grin.

'Won't be a surprise if I tell you, will it?' She darted away, clearly delighted with her plan.

Joe whistled cheerfully as he finished off the milking. He couldn't remember feeling happier in his life. His childhood days were fading into a dark memory. He didn't blame his parents for any of it, just circumstances that made life hard, but now, even when it was raining, life seemed better. He washed and changed his boots before going into the homely kitchen. Daisy was helping her mother bring supper to the table, a smile of pride on her face as she placed a large savoury pie on the table.

'I made it all by myself,' she announced. 'Mum's been teaching me how to cook and this is the first time I've made the pastry and everything by myself.'

'About time you were making yourself useful,' was all that Mr Baines could say.

Joe bridled at his words. It was unfair

of him as Daisy worked extremely hard in the dairy every day and for very long hours.

'I think it looks a fantastic pie,' Joe said warmly. He grinned at her, clearly showing her how much he approved of her actions. After all, when they were married she needed to be able to cook to look after her hard working husband.

'Let's be having it, then. See if you're anything like as good as your mother.' He sniffed. 'Smells right, any road.' He dug the knife into the crust and almost smiled his approval.

He served a piece of pie and handed the plate to Joe. The young man put vegetables on his plate and waited till everyone was served, his mouth watering in anticipation.

'That's wonderful,' he announced after his first mouthful. 'Well done, love.' His remark was met with a glare of disapproval and he realised he should never have used the familiar term.

'Don't you forget what I said, boy. Any of your silly ideas and you're off this farm right away. I won't have you looking at my girl with any of your wicked thoughts. She's a good lass and I aim to make sure she stays that way.'

'I'd never do anything to harm Daisy,' Joe protested. 'Really, sir, I think much too highly of her to cause her harm.'

'You'd better remember it, too.'

The meal was spoiled and Daisy's pride in her achievement was shattered. How could her father be so unreasonable? Joe was a good man and she believed her father had always appreciated the difference such a hard worker had made to his own life and the farm.

'I don't why you're so hard on Joe,' she ventured. 'He's never done anything to deserve you being so nasty to him.'

'You're just an innocent girl with fancy ideas in your head. You know nothing about the ways of the world and what men are capable of. If you let yourself be spoiled now, you'll never find a decent man to wed you.'

'But Dad, I've found the man I want to marry.'

'Marry? Rubbish. Get up to your room right away. I won't have this sort of talk at my table. You're nothing but a kid who hasn't even met a proper man. Joe here, he's nowt but a miner's son. Get off with you, girl.'

Daisy burst into tears and Joe sat shaking slightly at the show of temper. He didn't dare speak for fear of offending this man further.

'Now then, Dad,' Mrs Baines intervened. 'They've done nothing wrong. They're both young and of course they are going to like each other, living so closely as we all do. At least let Daisy finish her meal that she's taken such trouble to prepare.'

'I don't want to hear any more of this nonsense then. Come on then. Eat your food.'

Daisy slid back into her place and picked at the remains of her meal. She had lost her appetite, but she knew she would be in even more trouble if she failed to clear her plate. Her father never tolerated wasted food. She felt sick at heart and wondered however their problems would be resolved. Somehow, she had to talk to Joe again and make plans. His eyes wouldn't meet hers, as the meal was finished in near silence.

'You can clear now,' Mr Baines said as he put his knife and fork down.

Joe passed his plate and Daisy took it, not daring to look at him. It was going to be a difficult evening.

'I think I'll go and check on the stock,' he mumbled as he left the kitchen. He felt a bit mean leaving Daisy on her own with an angry father and anxious mother.

It was a situation that he simply couldn't handle and which had no obvious solution. Perhaps he could visit Nellie again when he had his next day off. At least talking about it to someone who wasn't involved, would be a relief.

Pressure Mounts

'I'm really worried about those two,' Nellie said over dinner the evening after their visit. 'Our Joe has a temper and I'm afraid he'll do something rash if he doesn't get his way.'

'I doubt the father will change his mind. You know these country types, once their minds are made up there's nothing you can do to alter them. But you can't do any more about it. They'll have to sort things out for themselves.'

'Oh I know you're right,' Nellie sighed. 'We've got our own problems to sort out. I'm planning to stay here in the morning and try to meet this cleaning woman. I'll come to the factory later if that's all right with you.'

'I suppose so. Yes, of course it's all right. We have to sort it out. But you do need to come in later. We have to agree on prioritising some orders. And I need one or two more ideas for the next season. Maybe something a little more conventional? The sales of the deco lines are going to peak soon and we have to be ready with the next *must have* styles.'

'Can we leave this discussion till tomorrow? I feel totally worn out this evening.'

'I suppose. But don't worry about your brother. He's quite capable of looking after himself. I'd talk to your mother, if I were you. She's a sensible woman. I'm sure she'll soon sort them out.'

Despite his suggestion and her feeling of tiredness, Nellie tossed and turned. She could sympathise with Joe. After all, it wasn't so very long ago that she was in a similar position herself.

At least James was better placed to look after them both, even though his parents had refused to accept her as his wife. Things had worked out well for them even though it meant that James had never been reconciled with his father before he had died.

It was never a subject that James would talk about and she suspected he held deep regrets about this loss. Joe was so happy in his farming life and looked better and more healthy than she has ever seen him look before.

She rose early and went down to the kitchen to make some tea. Nobody was up and sat by the stove, remembering her own days when she worked there. She remembered some of the bad times when she had felt bone weary and never seemed able to please anyone.

The good times had begun when James took an interest in her drawing skills, but that had led on to petty jealousies among the other staff and finally to her dismissal for a theft she had not committed. She must be absolutely certain she had found the real culprit for the current spate of thefts. She knew only too well what false accusations could do to a person. She heard someone coming along the corridor.

'Hello, Nellie. What are you doing here?' Ethel asked.

'I wanted a cup of tea. It was too early to wake anyone so I made it myself. I do still remember how to do it,' she added with a grin. 'Is your cleaning woman coming in today? Only I want to meet her myself.'

'Should be. About nine o'clock is her usual time. Is there something wrong?'

'I just like to know who is working in my home. Right, well I'll go and see if Mr James is awake and let the day begin.'

'I've been thinking about this head parlour maid idea.'

'Do you want to take that up?'

'For a bit, yes. Depends on who comes in as housekeeper. There's some as I can't work for. And you'll be taking on another maid as well?'

'I think so. We do value you, Ethel. But you really don't seem able to cope with all the accounts and everything else. I've got such a lot to do at the factory that I simply don't have the time to do it all myself.'

'Doubt you could do it anyway. You were just a maid here yourself, don't forget.'

'How could I forget it? But you have to accept that I am the boss now. I know it's difficult, but I try to be sympathetic to you all. It's hard for me, too, you must realise. James expects the house to run smoothly as it always has done. We shall be interviewing soon, I hope, so I'll keep you informed.'

Nellie felt that things were going to improve, especially in her relationship with Ethel. She went up to the nursery, where she could hear sounds of movement, and greeted her little son.

He seemed quite recovered from his illness and as lively as ever. She lifted him from his cot and he squealed with delight as she held him high and tickled his chubby middle.

'You're a smelly little thing, aren't you? You need your nappy changing, don't you?'

Jenny rushed into the room.

'I'm so sorry, Ma'am. I didn't wake up in time this morning.'

'It's all right. I was awake early and just thought I'd spend a few minutes with my little son.'

'I'll change him and wash him and then I'll bring him to you.'

'I'll help. I have done it before, you know.'

They spent a happy half-hour washing and playing with the little boy. Nellie realised how quickly he was growing and resolved to spend more time with him. She didn't want him to grow up knowing his nursemaid better than his own mother. The breakfast gong sounded.

'Thank you, Jenny. That was good to spend time with you both. I need to go now, though. A busy day ahead.' She went to the breakfast room and found James was already there.

'Hello, darling. I was wondering where you'd gone. You weren't there when I woke up.'

'I went to make some tea and sit by the fire.'

'Still worrying about your brother?'

'Well, yes. I talked to Ethel, too. She will be happy to stay on as head parlour maid, as long as she gets on with whoever we appoint as housekeeper. Then I went to the nursery and played with William for a while. I plan to spend more time with him in future. He's growing so fast.'

'Sounds like a good morning so far. Now make sure you eat something. You have a lot to do today and need a good start.'

'I'll just have some toast.'

'No, you won't. Have some bacon, and the eggs are good. I insist.'

She took a small helping, once more thinking how much she would have loved have food like this available in her past. In some ways, it didn't seem right to see so much food when she knew that others, not far away from here, were often starving.

Still, whatever was left over from their meals would be used by the other staff later in the day. Nothing much was wasted here, as she remembered from her days in the kitchen. They ate in silence, James glancing at his daily newspaper from time to time and reading out snippets of information, but Nellie wasn't really listening to anything.

'What's happening in the world doesn't seem to affect us, really, does it?' she said, thinking he needed a reply.

'I expect you're right. But I must get off to work or who knows what calamities might befall us. When do you think you'll be coming in to the factory?'

'I'm not sure. I'll walk in later, anyway.'

'I'd like you to phone me and I'll fetch you. It will probably be raining again and it's silly for you to get wet. We do need to have our meeting this morning. I want some of the sales staff involved as well.'

'I could come now if you prefer. See this Mrs Smith another time.'

'No, Nellie. It needs to be sorted out

as soon as possible. Besides, she might be warned off if you leave it. Ethel will tell her you want to see her and she might disappear altogether.'

James left and Nellie sat with a third cup of tea, waiting for the cleaner to arrive. She wanted to meet her before Ethel had chance to warn her. She stood by the window, looking along the road for signs of someone coming. A slightly familiar figure approached the house.

'I don't believe it,' Nellie murmured. 'She wouldn't dare.'

She ran down the stairs and burst into the kitchen.

'Florrie? What on earth are you doing here?'

'Nellie,' muttered the woman. 'I wondered how long I'd get away with it.'

'Florrie? Thought you said your name was Franny,' Ethel almost shouted. 'You said as how your name was Franny Smith.'

'Yes, well if they knew I was Florrie Thomas they'd have kicked me out

147

from the start. I'm a good worker, you know. I've changed a lot since the factory. Had to, didn't I? Hard times after you made them sack me.'

'You deserved it, Florrie. You never did much work. Spent most of the day flirting with Albert.'

'Yes, well, it was him I felt sorry for in the end. Did you know he had a wife and kids at home? He's never got another decent job since.'

'You didn't seem to have any sympathy or thoughts of his wife or children when you were flirting with him. It was common knowledge that you saw him outside work as well. So don't come all innocent with me. I know too much about you. Anyway, I want to speak to you privately. Come into my sitting room, please.'

Nellie left the kitchen feeling slightly nervous, but not daring to let anyone see it. Florrie was hard woman and she needed to know that she could get the better of her. She wished James was still here. He'd certainly take no nonsense from the woman. She sat down in the largest chair and indicated another chair for Florrie to sit down.

'Since you were employed here a number of items have gone missing. A woman answering your description took one of them into a pawn shop in town. Can you explain it?'

'What you accusing me of? I never did nothing like that. Never stole anything in my life. How d'ya know it was me and not one of the others?'

Nellie knew she was on difficult ground. She had no proof that Florrie was guilty. She took a deep breath.

'My husband and I have interviewed the rest of the staff and we are satisfied that none of them is responsible for the thefts. You are the only one we haven't spoken to.'

'Well, it isn't me what took nothing.'

'That means you took something,' she muttered, but it was lost on the woman.

'You jumped up bleedin' madam. Accusing me. You're just a miner's lass

149

and a cheap money-grabbin' girl who managed to catch a rich man.'

'That won't do you any good, Florrie. I am who I am and at this moment, I'm your employer.'

'If you think I'd stay here after this. You can stuff your job. Cheek of it.'

'Up to you. One way you can clear your name is to accompany me and my husband to the pawn shop. If the man recognises you, we shall know whether the accusations were false or not.'

Florrie opened her mouth to say something and thought better of it. Nellie kept her fingers crossed behind her back.

'So what do you reckon I took?'

'A silver tray for one thing and a diamond pendant.'

'Nah. Not me. What would I want with a silver tray?'

'The money it would fetch at the pawn shop. As it happens, my husband went and managed to buy it back. You told the shopkeeper it was a gift from a grateful employer but you'd rather have the money.' Florrie had the good grace to look away, the colour raised in her cheeks. Nellie continued, 'But the diamond pendant has never turned up. It belonged to my husband's late mother and was of great sentimental value.'

'Diamond, you say? Not just glass made to look like diamond?' Nellie shook her head. 'Worth much, is it?'

Nellie crossed her fingers again.

'No, mostly just sentimental value.' It was actually worth a great deal, but if she admitted that she stood no chance of getting it back.

'And would there be a reward for finding it?'

'You've got a cheek,' Nellie burst out. 'No, there's no reward. But if you admit the thefts and return the diamond pendant to me, I won't call the police. My husband would be furious if he knew I'd said that, but I needn't tell him. It's just an arrangement between us. Do you still have it?'

Florrie looked away. It was a good offer. If Nellie reported her to the police it would certainly mean a jail sentence for her. She'd been caught thieving once before and only just managed to get off with a caution.

A second accusation would do it, even if it wasn't proved. The pawnbroker would certainly be able to identify her. As for the wretched diamond thing, it wasn't much use to her. She had worn it once but thought it was just a pretty glass trinket. She should have known this little gold digger would have the real thing, even if wasn't worth a lot.

'All right. I have got your diamond and I did take the tray. Thought you'd never miss it with all the stuff you've got here. You did all right, you cheeky madam, didn't you? Managed to get yourself the top man in the company.'

'You're not off the hook till you bring the pendant back here. I'm going to ask someone to accompany you back to wherever you've left it and once I'm satisfied, you can go.'

'I suppose you won't be keeping me on?'

'What do you think?' Nellie said, only

just managing to keep her voice steady. She was almost shaking with anger. 'I'll see if Ethel can accompany you. If not, then you can do some housework while I call my husband. Mind you, I doubt he'll be quite so lenient with you. I suspect he'll certainly want to involve the police. Now, you have half-an-hour to return here with the stolen goods.'

'I've only got your necklace thing. The rest's gone.'

Nellie frowned.

'The rest?'

'Well, the tray, I meant.' She dropped her gaze rather shiftily.

'I suspect there was more that we haven't noticed. What else did you steal?'

'Nothing worth more than a few coppers,' Florrie protested.

'You'd better be right or I shall have revise my ideas about contacting the police.'

She rang the bell and Ethel arrived rather too quickly. She'd obviously been listening behind the door.

'I'd like you to accompany Florrie back to her home to collect some property of mine that she has confessed to having.'

'Right, Mrs. You're not fetchin' the police in then?'

'Not on this occasion, providing my pendant is returned in good order.'

The two women went out and Nellie heard the door slam and saw them walking down the road, seemingly without a care in the world. She hoped she hadn't been foolish in letting her off. It all seemed just too much trouble but she still had to explain it to James. She telephoned him to say she would be ready to go to the factory in an hour. His reaction to her handling of things was not good.

'You did what?' he shouted down the phone.

'Well, at least we're getting the pendant back. I thought this was the best way to ensure we had it returned.'

'But you hated that woman. You always said she was such a waste of time and a bad influence.'

'Oh, I don't know. I just feel I'm so lucky to have you and well, everything I do have. I don't want to send someone to prison, however much I was angered by her.'

'You're much too kind. She doesn't deserve it, but it's done now. We can't go back on our word. I'll see you soon.'

Nellie was on tenterhooks for the next half-hour. Suppose she didn't come back? Suppose she didn't bring the pendant back? James would be absolutely furious with her. She just hoped that Ethel was strong enough to make sure Florrie brought it back. She would have had further doubts if she could have heard Florrie questioning Ethel about the real value of the large diamond.

'If it's worth a few bob, we could sell it and split the proceeds. I could always say it had got lost. What do you think?'

'Don't push your luck Franny . . . Florrie. I reckon Nellie's been quite good to you not fetching the police. If Mr

James was around, he'd certainly have reported you.'

'Worth a try. So what's Nellie really like as a boss?'

'She isn't too bad, really. Doesn't know what the heck she's doing half the time. Mr James gets a bit mad at her when stuff goes wrong. Babby's sweet. She spends quite a lot of time with him. Better than most people with a nanny to do everything.'

'Right, then. This is it.' Florrie stopped outside a terraced house which she shared with her parents. 'I'll go and get this precious bit of jewellery and have done with it. You reckon I'll get my wages for this last week if I comes back with ya?'

'You might be pushing it. But you need to come back anyway. That's what she said.'

'Nah. Don't want to see her smug face again. I'll get the pendant thing and you can take it. And don't let on you know where I live.'

Ethel took the diamond back to the

Cobridge House and handed it to Nellie. She took it straight to her room and locked it in the drawer.

Ethel waited outside the room and spoke again as they went down the stairs together.

'Franny didn't want to come back with me, so I hope that was all right.'

'Florrie, you mean. Good riddance, I say. I suppose we'll have to find a replacement for her now. Oh dear, no sooner is one problem solved than another pops up to take its place. Thanks anyway. I have to go into work now so I'll see you later.'

James arrived as she was speaking and she went straight out to the car.

'I've got it back so that's the end of it. Now, what's the big problem you're so anxious about?'

'We'll talk when we get to work. They're all ready and waiting for us to get there. I've organised sandwiches so we can work through lunchtime.'

'It all sounds serious. Are we in trouble?'

'No, not really. Not if we make

proper provision for things that may be coming.'

The boardroom had several men sitting round the large table and they rose as Nellie and James entered the room. He signalled to them to sit and took his own place at the head of the table and Nellie sat on his right. It was all very formal and Nellie felt slightly nervous. It was not often that she sat in on these meetings.

'As you all know, we've been very successful with our art deco lines. They have been selling well and holding up against the competition.'

'That's right, but Clarice Cliff has certainly got the edge on us now,' one of the salesmen interrupted.

'You're right. And Susie Cooper started her new line with under-glazed colour banding and that is going really well. It's attractive and it's selling.'

'That's the one where they're painting lines of colour on the biscuit ware before it's dipped in glaze?' Nellie asked.

She wanted to be certain she was understanding everything as it was going to affect her whole method of working in future. 'I saw it in a magazine.'

'Correct.'

'But doesn't the paint sink in and run and spread out if it hasn't got the glaze to hold it? Like when you paint with watercolours and get the paper too wet?'

'Different paint thickness is used. Once it dries, it becomes just as stable. The advantage is that it misses out one stage in firing. Instead of firing the glaze and then decorating and firing again, once is enough. Think of the costs saved. They've done it before with the transfers. You must all be familiar with the blue and white various willow pattern designs?'

There was a murmuring of agreement round the table. Most of the sales team had been involved with manufacturing at some stage of their lives. James was proud of the family tradition that trained its staff thoroughly before sending them out on the road. This way, they could display proper knowledge of the ware they were selling.

'Some of that under-glazed pottery was wishy-washy, though. The colours were pale and a bit bland.'

'Yes, but with this colour banding, you get a modern look and bright colours. We shall be making a set of samples in the next week or two so you'll be taking them out soon. We're also reviewing some of the traditional sets and modernising these designs.'

'You're right, Boss. Some of the florals are simply not selling. People are choosing the things with cleaner lines. We need something between the busy looking Jazz styles and the old-fashioned roses and stuff.' The head of the sales team gained nods from the rest of the men.

'There you go, Nellie. Straight from the horse's mouth.'

'Right, well, it looks as if I have some work ahead of me. I'll get on it right away.'

'I think you need to do some research first. Spend some time looking round the stores and see what they are stocking. We don't want copies. Something original.'

'Shopping? Me?'

'Why not?'

'I'm too busy as it is.'

'Why not take your mother with you? Most women I know would be delighted to spend a day round the shops.'

The men round the table were laughing and mumbling that they wished their wives were equally reluctant to go shopping. Nellie was frowning and looked most uncomfortable.

'I'll speak to you later, James,' she said firmly.

There were a few smirks from the others. They had heard a lot about Nellie and her reputation as a tough nut had not escaped them.

'I think it's time we stopped for something to eat,' James suggested. He rang the bell at the side of the room and immediately, his secretary came into the room. 'We're ready for lunch now,' he told her.

Plates of sandwiches were brought in and a large pot of tea. The mood lightened and Nellie took James to one side.

'Do you need me here for the rest of this meeting? Only I have so many things to do, I really need to get on.'

'This is important stuff, Nellie. If you can't manage to do what you have to do, I keep telling you to get more staff involved.'

'You don't seem to realise I actually need time to find more staff for the house. After this morning's session with Florrie, I now have to find a cleaner as well. Honestly, James, you seem to have no idea of what goes on.'

'My mother always managed to run things smoothly.'

Nellie blanched.

'How could you, James? She didn't have to work in the factory. She also had the Dragon Lady to run the house like a well-oiled machine. And she mostly ignored you as a child. You said so yourself. Very well. I'll carry on sitting here and waste my time if that's what you want.'

She left him standing alone and got herself a cup of tea. Eating was out of the question as she would probably have choked. She felt near to tears. It was one of their first arguments in all the years. James must be worried or he would never had said those things to her.

'They're Hardly Speaking'

The tension from the day was apparent when James and Nellie arrived home that evening. Dinner was a sombre affair with little conversation. Doris went back to the kitchen after clearing the first course.

'Think they've had a row,' she announced to the others. 'They're hardly speaking and the Mrs has hardly touched her food.'

'Wonder what that's all about. I know she was worried about what the master was going to say about that Franny woman. He'd never have let her off.'

'I reckon she was just relieved to get her diamond back.'

'Take the pudding in. Maybe she'll like that better. Let us know the latest when you come back,' Ethel said with a giggle.

She knew the old order would never

have shown interest and Mrs Wilkinson would have kept them all in their place. But she was not Mrs Wilkinson and had even resigned as housekeeper. Still, until she was replaced, she needed to keep things going.

Doris returned.

'Still stony silence in there. There's trouble of some sort brewing. Just hope it doesn't land on any of us.'

'I expect it will blow over. Once we get a new housekeeper, things should be a bit easier.'

'Not for the rest of us. I bet it will go right back to us being bossed about. It's been great with you in charge, Ethel. A much easier life all round.'

'Think that's part of the problem. I never realised just how much there is to do. The accounts are in a right mess. I was never any good at sums. Didn't stay at school long enough to be able to add up properly.'

'You wouldn't think you'd have to do sums to look after a house, would you?'

'Seems like you have to do sums to

do anything these days.'

'Unless you're so rich you don't ever have to think about money,' Doris said with a sigh.

One of the reasons for the silence over their meal was that James was very concerned over a problem with the workers. This had taken up much of the afternoon meeting after Nellie had finally been allowed to leave.

It had long been known that many areas of the china industry involved harmful chemicals. Many workers had to leave work early due to sickness and lived out their final years in great discomfort. It seemed that attention was being given to these problems on a national scale. James had mentioned the afternoon discussion whilst they were dressing for dinner.

'So what is going to happen?' Nellie asked after they had eaten their pudding in another round of silence.

'I simply don't know. The factory owners have called a meeting next week to see what can be done. We stopped using some things like lead a while back, but the latest problem seems to be the use of flint in the bedding.'

'What's that?'

'Well, you know how there's a sort of powder put under the china to stop it sticking to the saggers in the kiln?' Nellie nodded.

She had seen the processes in the factory and remembered the dusty atmosphere when it was taken out of the large containers, or saggers, when it was fired.

'It seems that these workers are getting cancer and all sorts of other nasty lung diseases. They're trying to find something else to use instead of it. We've had a larger number of workers leave than ever.'

'I'm sorry to hear that. But I'm relieved it isn't me you're angry with. I'm sorry about my outburst today.'

'It wasn't helpful,' he snapped. 'I meant what I said, though. You have to get this house and staff organised. I can't be involved with managing that as well.'

'But you seem to expect me to manage it all and manage the decorating department, come up with new designs and look after our son as well. Oh yes, and spend a day looking round the shops. Thanks a lot, James. Very understanding of you. I'd better go to bed now so I can be up early and do a day's work before you even wake.'

She swept out of the room and went upstairs. She looked in on William and touched his baby soft cheek.

'My precious boy,' she whispered. 'Whatever happens, you will always come first. Sweet dreams.'

She undressed and got into bed. She felt tears pricking her eyes and tried to dry them before James came to join her. He seemed to be totally unaware of the strain she felt she was under.

He was not showing her any understanding and though she could put some of it down to his worries about the factory, she felt she was due some sympathy for her own problems. She lay awake for a long time and heard the hall clock chime eleven and then twelve o'clock and still James had not come to bed.

She slipped on her dressing gown and went downstairs to see if he was all right. But all the lights were out. There was no sign of him. Worried, she went back to their room and noticed a slit of light beneath the door of one of the guest rooms. Evidently James was sleeping there instead of sharing their own bed.

She finally cried herself to sleep. It was the first time they hadn't slept together when they were both at home. When she awoke, she had a headache and felt sick. Her father had always said she was crazy to marry out of her class. Should she give up and go back to her parents? Did she really want all of this? The house, servants, clothes, jewellery? She could take her little boy and go. But how could she deprive him of all the advantages this life could bring?

Besides, despite this sudden dip in her marriage, she adored her husband

and he had always said he loved her. Foolish thoughts, she convinced herself. Once the home problems were sorted out, life would get back to its wonderful normal routine.

She washed and dressed and went to look in on William. Jenny was dressing him and he gurgled with delight and chatted away in his own language. Nellie tried to engage with him, but her heart was too heavy and she said goodbye to him quite quickly.

In the breakfast room, James's place had been cleared and he had already left for work. Nellie poured some tea and ignored the cooked food left on the side. She was very concerned.

Never had they had a row that lasted more than a few seconds and never before had they gone to sleep with it unresolved. She had to decide what to do with her day.

She wanted to crawl back into her bed and try to get some proper sleep but it was not an option. Perhaps she should collect her mother and go to the stores to look at china, as James had suggested. But there were so many things she needed to do at home and at the factory.

'Do you want some fresh tea making?' Ethel asked as she came into the room.

'No, thanks. This is fine.'

'Should I get you some fresh toast then?'

'No, thanks, Ethel.'

'But you must eat something. Is there something wrong?'

'Nothing that need concern you.'

'But with the master going off early and I couldn't help noticing he slept in the guest room . . . '

'Don't tittle-tattle, Ethel. Don't forget I know only too well how people like to gossip. Have you done anything about finding a replacement for Florrie?'

'Course not. It was only yesterday, wasn't it?'

'Yes, of course. I'm sorry. But ask around and see if you can find someone. I'm hoping to be interviewing people for housekeeper in the next few days. I really need to get everything organised as soon as possible. I have work to do at the factory and can't be bothering with problems in this place.'

Ethel pursed her lips. She thought she could see where some of the arguments lay between Nellie and James. Wisely, she held her tongue. She felt almost sorry for her employer, recognising that she was finding her own life as difficult as she did in being housekeeper.

'I'm sorry I wasn't up to the job after you gave me the chance,' she said.

'That's good of you to say so, Ethel. It was also brave of you to admit that it was more than you could manage. I really hope you'll stay with us when we get someone else.'

'Thanks, Nellie. I'd like to, but it depends who comes.'

'I'll probably ask your opinion when I interview them. But don't tell any of the others I said so. In fact, keep it to yourself altogether.' James would certainly disapprove of the idea, she knew. 'And I don't object to you calling me Nellie when we're in private, but please don't do it in front of anyone else.'

'Right. Thank you very much . . . Nellie. I did know you as Nellie for quite a while, so it's sort of natural.'

When Ethel had left, she sat for a moment trying to decide what to do with the day. James had wanted her to go into town to look at what was for sale in the china stores.

She needed to do that before she started on designing new patterns, even if she did consider it a complete waste of time. But better still, she could call personally at the domestic agency and try to get the staff situation sorted. Just think, little Nellie Vale deciding to appoint household staff. It sounded very grand. Her decision made, she telephoned the factory and asked to speak to James's secretary.

'Please tell my husband I'm doing

the research he asked me to do. I won't be in today.'

What a pity I never had those driving lessons, she thought. It would take her hours on the bus to visit some of the larger stores, but it had to be done. She collected her coat and hat, told Ethel where she was going and set out.

There was a bus service close by and she didn't have to wait for too long. She began her day in Hanley, what was considered the main shopping centre. There were several large department stores there and she wandered around the china departments.

She was approached by the staff a number of times, but she told them all she was just looking. They all seemed rather superior ladies but she felt brave enough to ask a few questions.

'Do these designs sell well?' she asked looking at the work of one of Cobridge's main rivals.

'Oh, I really can't say,' replied one of the sales assistants rather snootily.

'Don't you know?' Nellie snapped.

'Only I don't want to purchase something that is less popular and have my guests talk about my lack of taste.'

She crossed her fingers behind her back so that it counteracted her fibs. It was something she'd always done as a child and it made her laugh inside. The expression on the woman's face changed immediately.

'Oh, I'm sorry, Madam. I thought you were asking for some other reason. We sometimes get spies from rival companies trying to find our best-selling items.'

Nellie blushed furiously. The woman had hit the nail right on the head. How perceptive of her.

'Perhaps I should go to another store and see if they are less suspicious,' she announced with as much confidence as she was able to muster.

'I'm so sorry, Madam. I didn't mean to offend you.' The woman was blustering and looking round anxiously in case her manager was watching. 'Please let me help you. What exactly are you looking for? Dinner ware? Tea set?'

'I think I have seen all I want to, thank you. Good day.' She left the department and smiled to herself.

She really wasn't very good at his. Their own home was full of Cobridge china and nothing else would ever be used there. Perhaps she needed to rely on window shopping. Or just give up and try to find the agency for domestic staff.

No doubt the woman running it would be just as superior as the lady in the china department. Well, she would show them she was just as good as anyone else. Probably better than most, she told herself.

She found the agency easily. It was a small office at the front of a house and not particularly imposing. Nellie felt more relaxed as she pushed open the door. A rather homely woman sat behind the reception desk.

'Good morning,' she said warmly. 'How can I help?'

'I need to appoint a new house-keeper, and also a maid and possibly a woman to clean. You know, the heavier stuff.'

'Certainly, Madam. Please take a seat and I'll write down a few details. Can I offer you a cup of tea while we talk?'

'How kind. That would be lovely.' Nellie felt very comfortable and knew she was going to be able to manage this interview. The whole prospect had loomed over her before and she had felt more nervous than if it was herself applying for a job.

'I'm Mrs Bentall. Now, sugar and milk?'

'Just milk, thanks.'

'Right now, let's get down to business. I've been working in domestic agencies for many years and decided to start out on my own, so I've plenty of experience.'

She began asking questions and making notes. Nellie was soon convinced that Mrs Bentall certainly had experience and knew exactly what she was talking about. She asked many things about the family, the staff kept at the house, the entertaining they did and about the house itself. Long after the second cup of tea had been offered and drunk, she finally stopped.

'Right, I think I have a fairly complete picture. Now I need to know what sort of person you want as housekeeper.'

Nellie was stumped for a moment. She wanted someone as organised as Mrs Wilkinson had been, but someone kinder to the other staff. She remembered acutely being terrified of the Dragon Lady when she had first arrived at Cobridge House. She tried to explain this and Mrs Bentall nodded.

'I have two ladies on my books whom I think might suit. Shall I ask them to visit you at home? It's usually the best way with my ladies. They need to see the premises and see you in your own environment. They are both available right away.

'As for the maid, I do have a rather

young girl who might just suit. I'll ask her to visit you at home too. I shall have to interview one or two other ladies for the cleaner position, but I am sure we shall soon find someone suitable. Now, we need to discuss remuneration and terms of living. I assume you have accommodation?'

Nellie passed on the details and suggested the wages they were prepared to pay. Thank goodness she and James had discussed this previously or she would have had no idea at all what to offer.

She felt quite exhausted after all of this and decided that she would return home rather than look at any more shops. The interviews were arranged for two days' time. As she waited for the bus home, she remembered the row she and James had. She had forgotten about it for a while and now she knew she needed to make it up with him. She got off the bus near the factory and went straight to his office. He was looking very strained and didn't seem best pleased to see her.

'What are you doing here? I thought you weren't coming in today.'

'You left without saying goodbye this morning and well, you didn't come to bed last night.'

'I thought it best. You were angry and I assumed you'd prefer to be left alone.'

'Well, you were wrong. I was very upset. I thought I'd let you know that I am interviewing domestic staff in two days so perhaps your precious routine will be less disturbed in future. I won't interrupt you any longer now. Oh, and staff in the stores are unwilling to let on what is selling well and what isn't. Afraid of industrial spies, I gather.' She turned to go, leaving her husband sitting at his desk looking somewhat disconsolate.

Nellie went along to her office near the decorating shop and looked in on Vera and the girls.

'Is everything all right here?' she asked.

'We're fine. Up to date with the

orders we've got, but we need to know what we're on to next. There's a whole load of the Jazz range ready for firing and a small order of the old rose tea sets.'

'I'm not sure what's on the books. I'll see if I can find out. Meantime, we need to try some new ideas. Colour banding on biscuit ware is the next big thing it seems.'

'What, painting on unglazed pots? That's different. Maggie's pretty good with banding. She's been doing a lot of the Jazz pots.'

'Good. I'll get some sent up. I think they want some of the larger jugs. For ornaments rather than as actual jugs, I gather.'

Nellie went back to her office and sat at the large drawing board. Just the smell of paint in the workshop had sent her mind flying in different directions.

Suddenly, she wanted to paint something herself. Not just designs on paper, but the real thing.

It was where she had started out with

her own brushes and paint tile for mixing colours. Perhaps she needed to work in with the girls for a little while, just to get back the feel and her love of the pottery she had always been so proud of.

She picked up her pencil and started sketching. Traditional. Modern. What was to come next? She had seen nothing inspiring on her trip into town, but then she hadn't really looked far. Perhaps something luxurious after the bold and audacious?

Coffee sets were popular. Small dainty cups for serving coffee after a meal were quite the thing. They had a range of them. Suppose they took one of the very simple shapes and painted an all over bright colour and then gilded the inside. A solid gold lining inside and bright glazed outside. A set of six with six different colours.

That was modern and used a line growing in popularity. It wasn't about to change their fortunes and would be expensive to make but then, something luxurious had been mentioned and this idea was certainly that. She would get a set made without saying anything and then show them to James and his sales team.

She went to the clay department and ordered a dozen or so coffee cups and saucers in the simplest shape they had and asked for them to be sent up as soon as possible.

After spending another hour sketching and achieving nothing new, Nellie decided to call it a day and go home. She hesitated about asking James for a lift home and decided to walk.

She felt totally exhausted after her lack of the sleep the previous night, her shopping trip and her futile attempts at thinking of new designs. Her mind was far too involved with her problems to allow her to think clearly. It was raining as she left the factory.

'Haven't you got a lift home, Mrs Cobridge?' George, the lodge-keeper, asked. 'Only you'll get soaked if you walk in this.'

'I don't think my husband is ready to leave yet.'

'I can send up and see. Why don't you shelter in the gatehouse just now?'

'It is raining rather heavily. Very well. Thank you.'

He pressed a buzzer and immediately one of the young lads came rushing across the yard.

'Go up to Mr Cobridge's secretary and ask if he's leaving soon as his wife needs a lift home,' George instructed.

'Right, sir,' the lad said and ran back into the building.

'Is he always waiting for you to buzz him?' Nellie asked. She had no idea that they had anything like this system in the gatehouse.

'I always has someone standing by in case there's any problems. And he opens the big gates when we have deliveries or send stuff out. I can't leave my post to do it, so we have a lad.'

'I see. Clever. So, how are you these days, George? I don't see much of you.'

'I'm all right. Now the kids have left

home, me and the missus are having a bit of a life of our own. Go to the flicks most weeks. She's got a real thing for seeing these films. That Clark Gable is her favourite. But she likes the others too. Romantic stuff. Anything that takes her mind off the Potteries. I try to tell her it isn't real, but you know what women are. Well, you would, being as how you are one.'

Nellie smiled, only half listening to what he was saying. Her mind was racing on. Films. Film stars. Romantic images. Perhaps this was something she could work on.

There were magazines published now with pictures of movie stars and articles about them. There must be some ideas there. She was just deciding to walk home and buy a magazine from the newspaper shop when the lad arrived back, panting from running all the way

'Mr Cobridge says he'll be down in a minute. Says you're to wait here for him.'

'Thank you. And thank you for the

shelter, George.'

'Glad to help. I remember when you used to come in every morning. Little scrap of a thing you were. And your mam was always bad in them days.'

They chatted comfortably for a while until James finally appeared and stopped the car beside the lodge. Nellie climbed in and thanked him for coming down so promptly.

'I would have walked, but I was very tired and I'd have been soaked.'

'I was nearly finished anyway. I have some papers to look at this evening, but it shouldn't take long.'

'I was fine waiting in the lodge. It was nice to catch up with George again.'

'What on earth could you find to say to him?'

'Plenty. I always used to have a few words with him.'

'Good heavens. You do surprise me at times. I don't think I even knew his name was George.'

'You should show an interest in the people who work for you. You get a lot of help from such folks in surprising ways. Mind you, there are people working here who have jobs I never even knew about.' James said nothing and looked strained. 'Is everything all right with you?'

'I'm tired. I'm still very worried about the future and how we can cope with the health problems that are being raised. I do care about our workers, but it seems that I don't care enough. Employment and working conditions seem to be a right these days rather than anyone being grateful they have jobs.'

'I think I can sympathise. I still remember the days when it was so cold you could barely feel your hands. We were lucky in the decorating shop. We could have fires when the clay end were practically suffering frostbite and the men loading the kilns had heatstroke.'

'That's the pottery industry.'

They parked in the driveway and Nellie dashed inside. Ethel greeted her and took her coat and hat.

'I'll get them dried for you,' she said.

'Thank you. It's a terrible evening. I'd like some hot tea sent to the drawing room, please. I expect Mr James will have some too. Oh, and I visited the domestic agency today. We shall be having two ladies coming to be interviewed for the housekeeper post the day after tomorrow. And a girl for the other maid. I hope she'll send someone for the cleaner job soon too. We should soon be back to being more organised.'

'What happened with that cleaner in the end?' James asked.

Nellie told him of the morning's events, knowing he would probably be angry that she had let the woman off. He was furious, but slightly mollified when told that the diamond had been safely returned.

'It turned out that it was the dreaded Florrie all the time. I couldn't get over her cheek. But she must have known I'd see her one day and recognise her. I did feel slightly sorry for her in the end, but

I was most anxious to get your mother's pendant back. I said it wasn't worth much more than sentimental value.'

'Good heavens. It's worth a small fortune.'

'I thought it might be but if she'd known that, she'd have pretended she'd already sold it. Now, I'm going to go and spend some time with William. I barely spoke to him this morning.'

James nodded and went to work in the library. Nellie gave a sigh as she went up to the nursery. She was still disturbed by the sudden lack of closeness to her husband.

She felt as if she was a failure as a wife and because of all the stress, her inspiration as a designer was also failing. At least she could be a good mother. She fixed a smile to her face and went into the nursery. She was too strong a person to think of giving up.

To Be Together

Joe had a day off. He planned to go back to see his parents and maybe Nellie as well. His mind had been churning over and over to think of ways he and Daisy might be together.

They found odd moments when they could speak in private, but Joe felt all the time that he was being watched. When he told Daisy he was going to see his parents the next day, she begged to go with him.

'How can you? Your dad'll never let you come out with me for a whole day.'

'I can say that I'm going to take the produce to the market. You could go off early in the morning and walk towards town and I'll drive the pony and trap and pick you up wherever you've got to.'

'But won't he be suspicious?'

'Probably, but there's nowt he can do

190

about it. I can say I want to do some shopping and come back late in the afternoon. You can go on to see your mum and then come back as late as you want. We can spend most of the day together. I only have to drop off the goods at the market stall and I'm done.'

'What if he finds out?'

'I don't care.'

Joe grinned.

'You're quite something, Daisy Baines. You'd do all that for me?'

'Course I would. I want to marry you, Joe. The sooner the better. Now you'd better go or he'll see us and spoil our plans for tomorrow. Don't remind him about your day off or he might smell a rat. I'll persuade Mum to let me take the produce tomorrow. She won't mind, I'm sure.'

Joe could hardly stop grinning for the rest of the day. He whistled as he went across the yard and was talking happily to the cows while he did the milking. He planned to get up really early the next day and leave the farm before breakfast.

He'd done it before on his days off. He had a long walk to get to the town and Mr and Mrs Baines knew he liked to spend as much time as he could with his family so they never commented. He even went to bed earlier than usual, but if he'd hoped for a decent sleep, he was disappointed.

A plan was forming in his head. It was a daring idea and he hoped Daisy would go along with it. He set out when it was light and walked along the lane towards the town. He didn't expect Daisy to catch up with him for some time and sat beside the road to rest. He wished he'd brought something to eat. He was starving, being used to a decent breakfast every day long before this time.

He heard a pony trap approaching and stood up. Daisy waved to him and pulled back the reins.

'I told my dad it was about time he thought of getting a little car. You should have seen his face,' Daisy laughed.

'I'm glad you got away with it. If this had been your mother, I don't know what she'd have thought. Do you want me to drive?'

'There's a sandwich on the seat. I thought you'd be hungry by now.'

'You clever girl. How did you manage that?'

'Said it was for my dinner. You'll have to make sure I don't starve come dinner time.'

'I expect our Nellie will give us something. Unless . . . well I've had an idea. I dunno what you'll say.'

'Better try me then, hadn't you?'

'I know it may not be the way you wanted it, but I wondered if we might get wed.'

'What?' Daisy pulled on the reins and stopped the pony in the middle of the road. 'What? Today? How can we?'

'Well, if we can't get wed today, we could get a licence or whatever it is you need.'

'I think we do have to get a licence. Well, I'm sure we do. Oh Joe, how lovely. If we get a licence, we can get wed soon and my dad can't stop us.'

'Let's do it then. I think there's an office just off the market place that does it. Will your stall lady look after the pony for a bit while we see about it?'

'There's a place to leave it anyway. My mum always does that when she goes shopping. She told me about it this morning. But you'll have to get out of the trap before we get there or she'll tell Mum about it when she sees her next week. Oh, Joe, I'm that excited.'

'Go on then, love. I'll wait for you outside the Market Tavern.' He leapt down from the trap and Daisy drove into the market place. He went along the street to where he thought the registry office was situated. It seemed an age before Daisy arrived, looking flushed and not a little anxious. He took her hand and led her into the office.

'We want a licence to get wed,' he

told the woman behind the reception desk.

'Oh, yes? And do you have your birth certificates with you? And I presume you have a letter of authority from your father?' she said to Daisy. 'You don't look twenty-one to me.'

'I'm not. I mean, not quite. I didn't know I had to have a letter from my father.'

'It's the law, I'm afraid.'

'But I'm over sixteen. I thought I could be wed when I was sixteen. My cousin was,' she said anxiously turning to Joe.

'Only with parental approval,' the woman insisted.

'He'll not give permission, will he, love?' Joe replied. Daisy shook her head miserably. 'Are there forms we can have?' he asked. 'Only if my sister looks them over, she can help us see what we have to do.'

'I'm afraid not. You come in for an interview and bring the documents you need and the registrar fills in what is necessary. Once the licence is issued, you can marry within a prescribed number of days.'

Disconsolately they left and walked down the street hand in hand.

'I'm sorry, love,' Joe muttered. 'I had no idea it was such a business. I don't even know if I've got a birth certificate.'

'And Dad keeps all our papers locked away in a strong box. He'd never let me have it for anything. Oh Joe, it's just not fair, is it? We love each other and want to be together, but everyone's trying to stop us.'

'Never mind. At least we've got the rest of today together. What do you want to do?'

'Maybe we could get the bus and go to see your mum? The pony and trap will be safe where it is for a bit.'

'All right then. It's only a short ride, but it'll be quicker than walking. I'd like to see our Nellie too, but she'll be at work.'

They caught a bus and arrived at the

Vale house just as Nan was making a pot of tea.

'Well, look what the wind blew in. Why didn't you let me know you were coming? I'd have got a bit of dinner ready for you.'

'It's all right, Mum. If you've got some bread we can make do with a sandwich. Cuppa would be nice, though.'

Nan was delighted to see Daisy again and asked a lot of questions about the farm and how Joe was getting on.

'And are you still walking out together? Course you are, or you wouldn't be here, would you?'

'Actually, Mum, we have a problem.' He explained about Mr Baines forbidding them to spend time together and the devious way they had organised this visit.

'That's terrible. Me and your dad were wed when we weren't much older than you two. We're all right still.'

'My mum and dad are the same. Only Mum lost a baby before me and it upset them so much they don't want to let me go.'

'What you going to do about it?'

'I don't know, Mum. He stops us even talking to each other if he sees us. We have to sneak out. We went to the registry office before we came here, but they said we can't marry till Daisy's twenty-one unless he gives permission.'

'Pigs'll fly before that happens,' Daisy said a little tearfully.

After tea and sandwiches, the pair decided that Daisy needed to set off back home. It would take her the best part of an hour and a bit to drive back and she had to collect the pony and trap first.

'I'll go back into town with you and then I'll try to catch Nellie after work. With a bit of luck, James will drive me back.'

They went to the bus stop and waited for what seemed a long time. Daisy insisted that she would go on her own so that Joe could go to see his sister.

'I'll call at one of the shops and buy

some ribbon or something just so they know I've been shopping.'

'You're a clever girl, Daisy. Take care now. I'll see you later.'

He waved as the bus drew away and walked along to Cobridge House. The car was parked outside so he knew they were back from work. He knocked on the door and Ethel answered.

'Oh, hello, Joe. Are you expected? Only the Mrs didn't say anything.'

'No, I just wanted to see her if she's in.'

'She's with the baby.'

'That's good. I'd like to see the little 'un.'

'You'd best come in. I'll tell her you're here.'

After a fair time spent chatting about the baby, work and so on, Joe got round to the main point of his visit.

'Were you twenty-one when you and James got wed?'

'I think so. Yes, I was, just about. Why?'

'So you didn't have to have a letter

written by me dad?'

'He didn't even know we were getting wed, did he? What's going on?'

'Me and Daisy want to get wed, but her dad won't even let us talk to each other on our own. We went to the registry place this morning but they said we have to have papers and letters from her dad if want to get wed before she's twenty-one.'

'Well you're both very young. Perhaps he thinks you don't know your own minds.'

'Oh, but we do. I've never loved anyone like I love Daisy.'

'Have you ever walked out with anyone else? I mean, how do you know she's the only one for you?'

'Same way as you felt about James.'

'But where would you live? What sort of work will you find to keep a wife and probably a baby one day?'

'At the farm, of course. They need us to keep it running.'

'You may be asking for a miserable life if you carry on this way.'

The arguments went back and forth for a long time and Nellie could see that there was nothing she could say to alter his mind. But equally, she could offer no real solution.

As time went on, she offered to give him dinner, though she knew James would not be pleased if they didn't dress for the meal as usual.

'Or are you expected back for your meal?'

'I don't know really. But if I've got to walk back, I should start out. It's a long way.'

'I expect you were hoping James would take you back?'

'Well it'd be nice, but I don't want to be no trouble.'

'I'll go and ask him what he thinks. He's working in the library. I shall be glad when I can drive and I shall be able to take you myself.'

Joe stood looking round the room. It was a very beautiful room with plenty of space, despite several large chairs and a couple of sofas. He could see why

Nellie had loved the fine china so much. It was colourful, but delicate and fragile looking. Wouldn't take much to break it, he thought.

He couldn't imagine eating food from plates like that with gold rims and painted flowers.

He heard his sister coming down stairs and turned as she came into the room.

'James says he'll take you back after we've had dinner. There's some sort of lamb dish tonight and Ethel's told Cook to put on extra vegetables.'

'Thanks, Sis. Thanks a lot. You've really done all right for yourself, haven't you?'

'I suppose so. It isn't always that easy, though. It was very difficult when we were first married and James's mother would have nowt to do with me. And sometimes, I feel I'm holding James back. There's things he'd like to do that I can't cope with.'

'But you're such a lady now. Servants and everything. You don't even have to go shopping or decide what meals to cook.'

'Oh, Joe, if only you knew. But let's not talk about it any more. Have you seen Mum lately?'

Dinner was a difficult meal with James preoccupied and Joe scoffing his food as if he hadn't eaten all day. Luckily, it was all over quickly and James drove her brother back to the farm.

He dropped him outside and left him to go inside alone. Had he known what reception awaited him, he might have accompanied his brother-in-law into the house.

'So, where've you been all day?' Mr Baines demanded.

'I went to see my mother and then my sister. I had dinner with them and James drove me back. Is there something wrong?'

'I'll say there is. You spent the day with my daughter, didn't you?' Joe blushed a fiery red and looked for Daisy to see if she might have some sort of answer.

'No use looking for her. She's in her room. After all we've done for you and everything I've said, you go against my wishes and slink off together. Well, that's it, my lad. You can clear off. I don't want you hanging round her any more.'

'I don't know what it is I'm supposed to have done, but you must know I'd never do anything to hurt Daisy. Not ever. I love her.'

'You don't know what love is, a lad of you age. You can stop the night, but I want you off the premises first thing tomorrow. Understand me?'

'Yes, sir. But I . . . '

'But nothing. Clear off.'

Silently and grieving inside, Joe went up to his room. He picked up his few belongings and put them together in a heap ready for the next day. He'd have to find a sack or something to carry them. It was going to be a long walk into town again and he'd have to stay at his mother's house.

There was room for him so it

wouldn't be so bad. But he'd have to find work again and that wasn't going to be easy without references. He lay on the bed and stared at the ceiling. He felt tears burning at the back of his eyes. No more Daisy. No cattle to look after. No more open-air life and great meals provided regularly. And how was Daisy? What had been said to her? How had Mr Baines found out about the day they had spent? They'd done nothing really so wrong, had they?

They'd scarcely even kissed each other except when she had left him at the bus stop. He heard Mr Baines go his bedroom. Mrs Baines must already be in bed as, he assumed, was Daisy.

Before long, he heard steady snoring and wondered if he dared creep along to Daisy's room just to make sure she was all right. But it wasn't worth risking.

He heard a noise outside and got up to look out. It was Daisy, standing on the grass beneath his window throwing pebbles up and missing by a mile.

'I'll come down,' he whispered. He crept out of his room as quietly as he could and down the stairs.

One of the steps creaked as he went down and he froze, but the steady snoring continued. He climbed out of the kitchen window to save opening the creaky back door. It was already open and obviously the exit that Daisy had used.

'What happened?' he asked when they had moved a little way from the house.

'He guessed what was going on. He made Mum tell him why I'd gone to the market and asked where you were. He was waiting for me when I got back and demanded to know where I'd been for so long. I tried to pretend but he was so angry, I broke down. I'm so sorry, Joe. He says you've got to leave.'

'I know. He told me to go in the morning. I don't know how he'll manage the farm on his own.'

'He says he'll soon get someone to take your place. But I can't stay here on my own. Can I come with you? Do you think your Nellie will give us a home? Like we planned. We could both work there.'

'I don't. You don't want to leave your home, surely?'

'If you're not here, then I don't want to be here either.'

'Oh, Daisy, love. I can't let you do that. We know we can't be married for a long time. And I'm not going to be with you unless we are married. It wouldn't be right.'

'I mean it, Joe. If you go then I'm leaving too. If you won't take me with you then I'll find some other way to be near you.'

'But, Daisy, I won't have a job or any money. Besides, how will your mum and dad manage without either of us?'

'P'raps they'll see how much both of us do every day to keep this place running. There's nothing you can say that will stop me. I'm coming with you and that's an end of it. I'll pack some things together and we'll go to the village and catch the bus to town first thing. We'll have breakfast and then set off after that.'

'I'm not sure they'll want to give me breakfast.'

'I'll cook it, then.'

'I'm still not sure, Daisy. How about I get something sorted and then send for you?'

'You can just shut up. I've decided and that's an end to it. Now, creep back to your room and don't make a sound. I'll follow you up in a bit. I can always say I was getting a drink of water if they hear anything.'

Scarcely daring to breathe, Joe crept up the stairs, trying to avoid the loose step.

He dreaded what they'd say if he'd been caught. He heard Daisy coming up the stairs and held his breath again. He heard voices but seconds later, he heard her door shut. It seemed they'd got away with their midnight tryst.

Neither of them slept for more than a few minutes. Daisy felt excited and scared at the same time. She'd never lived anywhere but the farm and the little she'd seen of other houses, everything was going to be strange and a great adventure.

She put a few clothes and other necessities into a bag and took it down early next morning. She hid it in the dairy so she could pick it up without raising suspicion when she went outside later.

She lit the range and put a kettle on top to make tea. It was always warm and was soon blazing. She set the table and wondered where Joe was. She'd expected he'd be down early before her father came in from milking.

Come to think of it, she hadn't heard him go out to start the milking. She went out to see if he was in the parlour but found Joe there, doing his tasks for what would probably the very last time.

'Your dad hadn't come down so I thought I'd make a start here,' he told her.

'That was good of you under the circumstances.'

'You can't leave animals to suffer. Oh, and I need something to put me things in. A sack or such-like will do.'

'I'll see what I can find.' She left him to his chores and went back into the kitchen. Her father came in.

'I'm late for milking. Bring me a brew out when the kettle boils,' he ordered.

'Joe's out there. He's nearly done. I'm cooking him some breakfast before he goes. Unless you've changed your mind?' she added hopefully.

'I want him off the farm right away. He can have some breakfast, being as he's done his work anyway and then he's to go. Understood?'

'Understood.' She dared not say anything else for fear she might let something slip. Her mother came in as Mr Baines left the kitchen.

'We're all behind this morning after the disturbance in the night. Are you all right, love?'

'I'm still upset. Sorry I woke you when I went to get some water.'

'Couldn't be helped. Your dad was worried you might do something silly.'

'Well, I didn't, did I? Now, I'll get on with the cooking, shall I? Joe's doing the milking so he'll want something to eat before he goes. And my dad wants a brew taking over. Will you do it or shall I?'

'If Joe's out there, I'd better take it. He'll sound off again if you two young ones are together.'

She cooked bacon and eggs and some wild mushrooms they'd gathered and put them in the oven to keep warm. Then she went upstairs and took her laundry bag up to Joe's room ready for him to pack his few possessions.

She saw his things on the bed in a heap and put them in the bag for him. She picked up his best jumper and sniffed his scent on it. Soon they'd be spending every day together, free to talk whenever they wanted and away from the fear of her father's anger.

He'd be furious when he discovered they'd both gone, but it was his own

211

fault for being so unreasonable.

She heard the back door rattle and went down to the kitchen.

'Your dad says I can have me breakfast then I have to go,' he told her.

'It's all ready for you, in the oven.' She put it in front of him and sat down with a plate of her own. 'I thought we'd better have a good feed before . . . ' she broke off as her parents came in.

She put her knife and fork down and leapt up to get their meals. They sat down without a word and ate heartily. She poured second cups of tea and when Joe had finished, he got up and went to his room.

'Have you paid him his dues?' Mrs Baines asked. Her husband glared at her. 'Well, it's only right he has the wages due to him,' she said firmly. 'He'll be out of work for a while, no doubt. And if he goes home, he'll need to pay board to his mother.'

'It's his own blasted fault. All right. I'll pay him up to yesterday.'

'And for this morning's milking.'

'You're barmy, woman. After what he's done to our girl?'

'He's done nothing. You know he hasn't. They're just young, like we were once. You've got a short memory, Tom Baines. Don't you even remember how you felt at his age? I was Daisy's age myself when we got wed.'

'And just look what happened. You lost a babby. Our son.'

'We've had a good marriage, haven't we? And a whole lot of people lost babies in those days. You had a brother yourself and he was lost.'

'Don't tell me as you'd let the lad stay after lying and cheating?'

'I'd certainly give him a chance. He's the best worker we've ever had here and I don't know how you think you'll manage everything without him. Our Daisy isn't strong enough to do his work and I'm not wanting to start working outside again.'

Daisy was listening without saying a word. Was there just a faint chance that her father would relent after hearing his wife's words?

'No chance,' he said at last. 'He'll only be lying again and still trying to do his worst to our girl. I'm not having it. I've made my decision and that's it. I'll pay him his dues and that's all.'

He rose from the table and went to his desk. He unlocked his money box and extracted some coins. He put them in an envelope and gave it to his wife. 'You can give him this. I don't want to see his lying face again. I'm going out and want him gone when I come back in.'

Daisy cleared the table and began the washing up. She felt tearful now things had come to this point. She heard Joe coming down the stairs and dried her hands. Her mother was waiting for him with the envelope of wages and she handed it to him.

'I'm sorry, lad. I tried to make my husband see sense but he wouldn't budge. You've been a good worker. I could send on a reference if it's any use. Leave me your mum's address and I'll see what I can do.'

'Thanks; Mrs Baines. I've loved being here. I love the animals and even though it's sometimes hard going, I enjoyed the work in the open air. I've never been so well fed as I have since I've been here. Thanks for everything.'

He carried his bag out, hoping Mrs Baines didn't realise that it was Daisy's own laundry bag he was using. She followed him to the door.

'Wait down the lane,' she whispered.

Her mother assumed her daughter's slightly red eyes were because Joe was leaving. The girl gave her mother a hug and dashed up to her room. Mrs Baines said nothing and shook her head gently.

She had great sympathy for both of them. She went to the sink and finished washing the pots. She didn't hear Daisy slip out of the side door and didn't see her leaving, wearing her best coat.

The girl picked up her bag from the dairy and kept her fingers crossed that she didn't bump into her father. Quickly she went through the main gate and ran down the lane, not slowing until she knew she was quite out of sight of the farm.

Moving On

Joe was waiting for her near where the lane joined the main road. They walked hand in hand, saying nothing until they reached the edge of the village.

'There should be a bus soon. There's usually one at half-past.'

'Sooner the better,' Joe muttered nervously. 'Once they realise we've both gone, they'll be after us.'

'Mum won't say owt for a bit. She thought I was upset at you going and left me to go to my room. I was a bit tearful. It isn't every day you leave home.'

'You're really sure this is what you want?'

'Course I am. I'm here, aren't I?'

'We don't even know where we're going.'

'I thought your sister's would be the best bet. They've got plenty of room there and I reckon I could help her round the house. Maybe you could help in the garden.'

'They've got a gardener and they're getting new staff. Housekeeper and a maid. Nellie told me when I was there yesterday.'

'Well, if they haven't got them yet, maybe I can be one of them.'

'She wouldn't like my girlfriend being a maid. Wouldn't be right for the others. No, I think we'd best go to Mum's to start off. See what she says.'

'Here's the bus coming now,' Daisy said with a feeling of relief. She'd been dreading the clip clop of horse's hooves on the road if her father came after her. They waved for it to stop and Joe paid their fares.

'Bit quicker than the pony trap yesterday,' Daisy said as they arrived in the town.

'Give me your bag. I'll carry it for you. It's a long walk up the hill. Second time in only two days. I hope you know what you're doing.'

'Course I do. I shall worry a bit about my mum though. She was finding the dairy hard work on her own before I took it on. You know, with the cooking and everything else.'

'She won't have to cook so much if we're not there.'

'My dad will expect meals as usual. It's not that much extra work to make meals for more people. Anyhow, they'll have to take someone else on. Dad can't manage everything himself.'

'Well, whoever they find, I just hope he isn't as good as I was.' They both laughed, relieving what was growing tension.

'What do you reckon your mum's going to say?'

'She'll be all right. My dad might kick off, though. He hates anything being changed in his life. Just a good job they don't still live in that poky little house where we used to live. We'd have been camping on the doorstep.'

Nan Vale was busily cleaning when the pair knocked on the door.

'Whatever are you two doing here again?' she asked, looking somewhat perturbed. 'Is everything all right?'

'Not really,' Joe began.

'Well, you'd better come in. Don't trip over the mop. I'll put the kettle on and you can tell me what's wrong. Come on, love. Sit down by the fire. You look a bit chilled.'

'Thanks, but I'm all right really. I'm just tired. Didn't get much sleep.'

Joe explained what had happened while Nan was making the inevitable pot of tea. She listened without making any comment, nodding and frowning at some points.

'I see, and so you took it on yourselves to run off together. So how's that going to work? You can't get married without your dad saying he'll agree and he isn't going to do that. Where do you plan to live and how will you manage for money?'

'I wondered if we could stay here? Or at our Nellie's?'

'Your dad'll never let you both stay

here. I dare say you can stop here, Joe, but he won't have Daisy under the same roof, not unless you're wed.'

'We'd best go and see Nellie, then.'

'I wondered if Nellie would give me a job. I'm quite a good cook now and I could help with the housework and the baby,' Daisy said.

'I suppose you could ask, but I can see that might be difficult. You being practically family and all.'

'And maybe I could do some gardening for them. I've learned a lot about growing stuff. They might like to have some hens as well. I can look after them as well.' Joe was sounding enthusiastic and about to suggest keeping a cow as well and possibly a goat but thought better of it. It was a town, after all.

'You'd best go round to Nellie's house, then. I'm not sure if she's at home today or if she'll be at the factory. She said summat about interviewing someone for the housekeeping job. I think that was today.'

'Well, you better have something to eat here and then walk round. I don't know. What a mess. I can see why you wanted to leave, but I don't think you've really given it a lot of thought. You're a daft pair. But I think your parents are going to be very angry. Do they know where we live?'

'Not exactly,' Daisy replied. 'But they do know Nellie works at the Cobridge factory. Well, that they actually own it, I suppose.'

'So that's where they'll come looking for you?'

'If they bother to come after me at all. I think they might disown me now, anyway.' Daisy felt tears pricking at the back of her eyes. Though this was her choice and she'd do anything to be near Joe, she couldn't help feeling upset that she'd left her home and everything she'd always known.

'There, there now, love,' Nan said gently. 'I'm sure it'll all come out in the wash. I'll just have to pop out to the shop and get something to feed you on.

I haven't got much in. You just sit there and try to work out what you're going to do.'

They sat side by side, clutching each other's hands. Now they'd taken the action, it didn't seem quite so straight-forward. Neither his parents nor sister were going to agree to have the couple to stay under the same roof, despite the fact they had actually been doing so for the past couple of years. It was all different now. They had declared their love for each other and that changed everything.

'You know it isn't too late for you to go back home, love.' Joe could see how troubled Daisy was feeling.

'It is too late, Joe. Anyway, I really do want to be here with you. We've made our plans and even if we have to wait forever to get married, at least we can see each other every day and spend time together. If I go back home it'll be like being in a prison. I'd have to lie all the time just to get out of the house. I can't live like that.'

'If you're sure. We'll go and talk to Nellie this afternoon. At least she'll have a bed to offer you, all them spare rooms they've got.'

Nan came back with slices of pork pie and some fresh rolls. Daisy helped set the table and chatted to Nan while Joe took his bag upstairs. He came down and asked,

'Am I to share with Billy?'

'You'll have to. I kept your old bed. I'll find some sheets for it later. I suppose if our Nellie can't put Daisy up, she could share with Lizzie for a bit. I'd have to get another bed or mattress on the floor. Nellie always shared a bed with Lizzie, but I couldn't expect Daisy to do that. But like I said, your dad won't have both of you staying here.'

'Thanks anyway, Mum. It's all happened so quickly with me being chucked out. And you know I'd never do anything to hurt Daisy. I don't know what Mr Baines thinks we've done but I assure you, we haven't.'

'You're a sensible girl, Daisy. Our Joe

has made a good choice and I'm sure it'll all sort out in the end. Come on now, let's get ourselves wrapped round this pork pie. I'll pour some more tea too.'

When the meal was over, the young couple left Nan and went round to see Nellie. It was a repeat of the journey of the previous day. Again, Ethel answered the door.

'You here again? You can come in, but you'll have to wait. The Mrs is seeing a woman about the housekeeping job. You'd best go to the morning room. She's in the drawing room.'

'Nice to have a choice, isn't it?' Daisy said politely.

'So, what's she like, this woman?' Joe asked.

'Bit of a hard nut as far as I can see. I reckon she'll win out over the one as came this morning. She was nice, but I think the Mrs will want someone a bit bossier. Shall I fetch you a cuppa?'

'Not for me, thanks. We've been drinking tea all morning with Joe's mother.'

'So, what brings you back again so soon?' Ethel asked, her curiosity getting the better of her.

'Something we need to talk about to my sister,' Joe said. He didn't want her gossiping to the others. He remembered Nellie's tales of what went on in the servants' quarters.

This was what worried him about Daisy being part of the household staff. She'd be a mixture of family and staff and it might become difficult for her.

'Right, well I'd best get on. I'll tell the Mrs you're here when I get the chance.' She left them and Daisy wandered round the room looking at the pictures and touching the pieces of furniture.

'What a pretty desk this is. I expect James's mother used to sit here and write her letters.'

'Maybe. Doubt our Nellie uses it much. Don't suppose she ever writes letters. There's nobody to write to. Fancy having a room just to have breakfast in. It's as big as the whole downstairs of the place we used to live. Must have bin a great big change for our Nellie when she came to live here.'

'Do you think we'll ever have a place of our own?' Daisy asked.

'I s'pose we will. One day. I always thought as we'd live at the farm. Or somewhere near there. Maybe we'd find a cottage.'

In the drawing room, Nellie was trying to remember if she'd asked all the questions James had told her to ask when interviewing the two ladies. She had hoped that he would be present at the interviews, but he had meetings to attend and so it was left to her. She was anxious not to make a mistake and found the whole business a great trial.

'Well now, Mrs Marsh, is there anything you'd like to ask me?' she asked finally.

'I would have complete charge of the staff, should I wish to take the post?' she asked brusquely. Nellie was suddenly reminded of the Dragon Lady and gave a slight shiver.

'Oh yes, of course. I should rely on you to organise everything. As I said, I have important work at my husband's factory and I don't have enough time to do much at home. What little spare time I do have, I like to spend with our son.'

'That's agreeable to me. I don't like interference with my methods of working. Very well. I should like another look at the kitchen and my accommodation and then I'm done.'

Nellie felt warning bells ringing. The woman seemed to assume she had got the job and she was unsure of how to tell her the decision was not yet made. Though she wanted to be able to leave the work to someone else, she did not want to find she was being bullied again.

'As I said at the beginning, there are other candidates for the post. I shall let you know if you are the successful applicant in a day or two.'

'I'm not certain that this post will suit me,' she replied with a sniff. 'I'm not used to the lady of the house being a working woman.'

Nellie smiled. Her decision was already made. Though the woman she had interviewed during the morning was less forceful, she would be a much kindlier soul to have about the place.

'I'll take you to the kitchen if you wish,' Nellie told her. They left the room and went along the corridor. She heard voices in the breakfast room and opened the door and looked in. 'Joe. Daisy. What are you doing here again?'

'We need to talk to you, Nellie. Got something to ask you.'

'Just wait a while. I must show Mrs Marsh out. I'll be back soon.' She closed the door and frowned.

She had a suspicion that she already knew what they wanted to ask. 'Sorry, Mrs Marsh. You wanted to see the kitchen again?'

'Don't bother. I doubt you'll suit me. I like things more ordered than this house seems to be. I run things differently and I doubt you and I would get on for long.'

'I see. I'm sorry your time has been wasted, but thank you for coming to see me. I wish you luck in finding something suitable for your talents. I'll see you to the door.'

'I'd have expected your maid to do that.'

'I'm here now. Goodbye, Mrs Marsh and thank you again.' The woman merely nodded and sniffed her disapproval. 'Good riddance,' Nellie muttered under her breath.

It was amazing how much she was reminded of the Dragon Lady, especially on the day she had first come to the house as the lowest of the maids. But on the whole, Mrs W had been worth her weight in gold.

Ethel had been bobbing around the darkest corner of the hallway and now she came forward. 'Did she get the job?' she asked.

'No. I think we'll have Mrs Potts from this morning. She may not have been quite such a bossy woman, but I think this one would have driven us all mad.'

'Eh, thank goodness for that. We were dreading you choosing her. We all liked Mrs Potts. Oh, your brother and his girl are here. They're in the breakfast room.'

'Yes, thank you. I saw them on my way down.'

'Only I put them in there cos you were in the drawing room.'

'Yes, thanks, Ethel.'

'They didn't say what they wanted.'

'No, that's fine, Ethel. I'll go to them now.'

'I did offer tea, but they said as they'd been drinking tea with your mum all morning.'

'Very well, thank you, Ethel. You can go back to your work now. I shall want you to get everything in order to hand over to Mrs Potts, so you'll have plenty to do. Then I must telephone the agency and pass on my choice. Always something to do, isn't there?'

Ethel was certain there was something going on and was longing to know exactly what it was. Nellie used to talk about her brothers and sister when she was a maid and Ethel felt she was entitled to hear it, whatever it was.

She went back to her sitting room, as long as it was hers. It would become the domain of Mrs Potts very soon . . . not that she minded too much. She would be glad when all this list-making and bookkeeping was someone else's problem. Besides, she had somewhat missed the companionship of the other maids when she sat in her exclusive little room.

Nellie went to the breakfast room.

'So, what's happened?' she asked.

'Mr Baines was furious that we'd been out together for the day and sacked me on the spot. Sent me packing.'

'And I decided to come with him. We know we can't get married for ages but at least if this way, we can see each other every day. What we wondered is whether you will give me a job of some sort and let me stay here?'

'And I could come and do the garden for you and stay at Mum's. My dad won't let us both stay together and I don't suppose you will, either.'

'Are you sure you've done the right thing, Daisy? I mean, you were working at the farm as well as Joe and haven't you left them in the lurch?'

'Well, yes, I know. But if my father wasn't so pig-headed, it would never have happened. All we did was have the day together.'

'But you lied about it, didn't you? And you went to see about getting married. No wonder he was angry and probably very worried.'

'I thought at least you'd see our point,' Joe said angrily. 'I'd have thought you of all people would be sympathetic.'

'I am sympathetic, but I'm not sure what's the right thing to do. Of course you can stay here, Daisy, for a little while. But I can see you both need to earn money and it just wouldn't work, you being part of the staff here in the house. I suppose I might find something in the factory. I'll think about it. As for gardening, the same thing applies to you, Joe. I can't have my own brother labouring for me.'

'It's not as if I'd be inside the house. I'm good at growing stuff. And you could get some hens. Fresh eggs for the little lad. Just the job, I'd say.'

'Oh, Joe. For how long would that work? I couldn't pay you enough to let you save up to get married. It would just be enough for you to pay some board to Mum and Dad.'

'But Nellie, we have to do something. Please help us.'

'I can't go back home. If I did, I'd never be able to see Joe again and that would break my heart.'

'Oh, dear. I don't know what to say. All right. Daisy can stay here and we'll find something for her to do. You can do some gardening, just for a few days mind, till we think of some way round all this.'

'Thanks, Nellie. I knew you wouldn't let us down.'

'Yes, thank you, Nellie. We won't ever forget this.'

'Right, well, I'd better get someone to fix up a room for you. We'll go and see Mum and sort out how it will work. Then you'd better both come back here for dinner. Have you got any luggage, Daisy?'

'Just this bag. I didn't bring much cos we had to carry it all and I didn't want Mum or Dad to see me.'

'Right. Well, maybe you can borrow some of my things until we get everything properly arranged. We're about the same size.'

There was a great deal of discussion over the meal that evening. James was not pleased with the new arrangements and voiced his concern when he and Nellie finally went to bed. He raised all the points that had concerned Nellie, especially anxious that they took account of the fact that nothing could be permanent.

'I know,' Nellie agreed. 'It's all temporary. That girl will hate living in the town and she'll soon miss her parents and her life on the farm.'

'Is love enough to change her life for good?'

'It was for me,' Nellie smiled as she snuggled closer to her husband.

A Farm Accident

For the next few days, Joe came to work in the garden. The old gardener was delighted to have someone to do the heavy work and exploited the lad dreadfully. Joe didn't mind as he simply wanted to prove himself useful to Nellie and James.

As for Daisy, she found herself various tasks to do. She mostly helped the cook, who was delighted to share her work with a willing pair of hands.

'You're a good girl,' she told Daisy. 'You've got a light pair of hands for pastry. How long do you think you'll be staying?'

'I'm not sure,' she said. She knew in her heart it could never be a permanent arrangement, not least because the other maids and Ethel were not exactly friendly.

Jenny, who looked after the baby was

all right but even she was a bit apprehensive about her own future if Daisy was here for much longer. She and Joe met up for lunch and went for long walks every evening. After another week, she told him she was going to write to her mother.

'I just want to be sure that she's all right. I know my dad can have a terrible temper at times and I don't want him taking it out on her.'

'Shall you tell them where you're living?'

'I'll have to. Otherwise she won't be able to write back to me, will she?'

'Why don't you go and visit them for a day? They can't lock you away now, can they?'

They discussed it with Nellie and she agreed it would be a good idea.

'For your own peace of mind, you need to know they are managing.'

'I don't what I'll do if they aren't managing, though,' she murmured. 'I think I'll just write a letter for now. They'll guess that I've come here, anyway. Would it be all right if I gave Mum this telephone number? She could always call if there was an emergency. There's a telephone she could use in the village.'

'Of course you can. There's always someone here to answer it.'

Daisy wrote a carefully worded letter, telling her mother that she was fine and being well looked after. She made sure she told her that she was staying at Nellie's house and that Joe was at his mother's home. That way, there could be no doubt in her mother's mind and hopefully, she would reassure her father. She posted it and waited anxiously for a response.

The new housekeeper, Mrs Potts, had moved in and everything was changing, hopefully for the better. Ethel had moved back into the maids' room and taken over her lighter duties once more.

Though she missed being a sort of boss, she was not sorry to lose the responsibility of the dreaded books.

Mrs Potts had been shocked by the muddle and insisted that Ethel spend some time with her trying to get them back into a proper order.

Fortunately, Nellie was not involved and though Daisy gathered something of the problems, she wisely chose to say nothing. The others were suspicious enough of her, knowing she was almost family. She got on well enough with Cook and tried to stay out of the way of the others by helping in the kitchen. At last a letter came back from her mother.

Dear Daisy.

Thank you for letting me know you're all right. I can't say the same for here. Everything is really difficult. We took on a new lad, but he isn't half the worker your Joe was.

I'm finding the dairy very hard work and your dad expects his meals on the table at the usual times. I don't know how he expects me to do everything by myself. Please won't you come back? I miss you some-thing terrible.

Your loving mum.

P.S. Thanks for giving me the telephone number.

It did little to make Daisy feel any better. She showed the letter to Joe and to Nellie.

'Nice to know your mum appreciated me at least,' Joe said. 'So what are you going to do?'

'I'm going to write again and say I'll come back if Joe comes as well. Maybe my dad'll realise I mean what I say.'

'I doubt his pride will allow him to give in,' Nellie suggested. 'But it's worth a try.'

Daisy agreed and wrote again. The reply came back a few days later.

'*Your dad won't budge. But please come and just see us anyway.*'

'I think you should go and see them,' Joe told her. 'You need to keep in touch with them and let them see for themselves that you're well and that you really mean what you say.'

'All right. I will. I won't tell them I'm coming, though, and then they won't be all on edge.'

Her trip was arranged for the next day.

'I'll be back in time for supper, if that's all right,' she told Nellie.

'Joe had better come, too, then we can hear how it all went. James has a meeting tomorrow evening so we'll be quite casual and he won't insist on us dressing for dinner,' she said with a laugh.

It had always been difficult when Joe and Daisy ate with them as neither of them had the sort of clothes that James seemed to expect as being appropriate dress for the occasion.

'You've been a proper brick, Nellie,' Daisy told her and gave her an emotional hug. 'I don't know what we'd have done without you.'

'It's all right. But you will have to make some sort of permanent arrangements before too long. Joe needs a proper job and you need some way of earning money.' The arrangement had been that Daisy helped out in return for her keep, but she had refused to take any proper pay.

Joe walked her to the bus stop early next day before he started work in the garden at Nellie's.

'Be strong, love. Don't let your dad bully you into anything.'

'I won't. I'll see you tonight. And don't worry about me. I'll be fine. I love you, Joe.' She reached up to give him a peck on the cheek as the bus drew to a stop.

He waved as the bus drew away and crossed his fingers that all would go well for his girl.

Daisy sat quietly looking through the window. It was only a half-hour journey and she found the change from the black surroundings of the town to the green of the countryside quite remarkable, in so short a distance.

She got off the bus in the village and walked down the lane to the farm. She felt strangely nervous as she neared her home and stopped to look over a gateway, wondering how she would be received. She walked on and pushed the familiar yard gate open.

It was quiet and nobody came out to greet her. She looked into the dairy expecting to see her mother working, but she was not there. She pushed open the kitchen door.

'Mum?' she called. 'Are you inside?'

'Daisy? Oh, Daisy. It's so lovely to see you. Are you all right? I mean, have you come back to us?'

'Just thought I'd come over for the day.'

'Oh, come here, love. Give me a hug. You're looking pale.'

'Well, I'm not working outside much so I expect that's why. How are you really, Mum?'

'I'm all right. Just tired, like I said in my letter. And I do feel a bit lonely. Your dad never says anything much. And the new lad is thick as two short planks. He doesn't ever have anything to say. Just shovels his food down at every meal and then goes to his room. I must say I miss having someone to chat to.'

'I'm sorry, Mum. I'd come back . . . we'd both come back like a shot, but only if Joe can come as well.'

'You're dad's fixed on that one. I'll put the kettle on, anyway. We can have a proper talk before your dad comes in. I've got a pie for dinner so there's plenty to go round.'

It felt surprisingly comfortable sitting in the kitchen next to the range. Everywhere was spotless as always and the smell of food cooking seemed comfortingly familiar. They drank tea and ate a piece of homemade short-bread each.

'Shall I help you in the dairy?' Daisy offered. 'I expect you've got to make butter for market.'

'Blast it,' her mother replied, most unusually for her. 'I've only got you for a day, after all. The butter can wait. I want to make the most of having you here.'

Her daughter shrugged. She just hoped her father didn't take it out on her mother after she had left. She relaxed and they chatted comfortably. She told her about the big house and about the other girls who worked there.

'They're not quite sure how to take me. They think of me as being part of the family, but not quite. I mostly eat with them in the servants' dining room. James insists they dress for dinner and I don't exactly have the sort of clothes for that. By the way, would it be all right if I take some more of my things back with me tonight? I couldn't take much before when I left.'

'Course you can, love. Only it all sounds a bit more permanent that we'd have liked to think. What do you intend to do eventually?'

'We want to get wed as soon as we can, but I can't. Not without a letter signed by my dad. Not until I'm twenty-one anyway.'

'I will try to make him see sense. I can see you've got your heart set on this lad. I can also see you could do a lot worse. Now I've realised what a good worker he is, I have a lot more respect for him.'

'Oh, Mum, if only you could persuade Dad.'

'Persuade him to do what?' a loud voice said from the kitchen door.

'Hello, Dad. How are you?'

'What are you doing here? Turfed you out, has he?'

'Course not. I came to see how you both are.'

'Well, you're not welcome here. Not without an apology and a promise that you won't see that waste of time again.'

'I'm sorry you were upset, but Joe and I are always going to be together.'

'Then you'd best get back to him. You're a harlot and no daughter of mine. Don't know how you've got the face to come back here when you're living in sin with some lad.'

'I'm not, Dad. I'm not living with Joe. We've never done anything wrong. Truly we haven't. I'm stopping at his sister's and he's living with his parents. But we can at least see each other every day and we don't have to hide away somewhere if we want to have a conversation.'

'Don't you see, you stupid girl? All he wants is to get his hands on this farm. He thinks if he can get his feet well and truly under the table . . . our table, he stands a chance of inheriting this farm and the land. He's no good to you.'

'Oh, and what do you think will happen to this farm when you go? Who do you think will inherit it?'

'I did think you'd find a decent chap. Another farmer, perhaps. Someone with property of his own.'

'Not many of them around are there?'

'There's Ashton next door. He's got a decent farm of his own.'

'But he's a widower. He's an old man, nearly as old as you are. I would never marry anyone like that.'

'I'm not an old man. Nor's he. You could do a lot worse.'

'Oh, for heaven's sakes. Just listen to the two of you,' Daisy's mother interrupted. 'Daisy has got a decent lad who she wants to marry. How could you even think she'd be interested in old man Ashton? Besides, he's got two married sons of his own. I'm sure he'd love to add our farm to his own to leave to his sons. They'd have a place each, then, wouldn't they? Where would our Daisy be in that little plan?'

'Nowhere, cos I'd never let it happen,' Daisy almost shouted. 'Oh, this is useless, Mum. I just wanted to see how you were cos I was worried about you. I'll go now.'

The door opened again and a spotty-faced young lad came in.

'Is it dinner time?' he asked. 'Oh, have we got company?'

'This is my daughter, Daisy. This is Terry. I've got to put some carrots on and then dinner'll be ready.'

'Hello, Terry,' Daisy said as she got up from her seat. 'I'm just leaving.'

'You're having some dinner first,' her

mother said firmly. 'I'm not letting you go away hungry. Don't listen to your father.'

'If you're sure. Shall I set the table?'

'Thanks, love. You two men can go and wash your hands, ready.'

It was a difficult meal. The two women tried to chat, but Mr Baines made the tension almost unbearable. Terry shovelled his food down just as Mrs Baines had said and he got up and left the table as soon as he had finished. No thanks and no waiting till everyone had finished.

'Is he always like that?' Daisy asked. Her mother nodded. 'I'm surprised you haven't said anything. You were always hot on good manners.'

'To be honest I'd rather see the back of him. It's a relief when he goes. Now, do you want a cuppa?'

'Hasn't she got to be on her way back to her other life?' Mr Baines suggested.

'She can have some tea first.'

'Up to you. I've got work to do.' He stamped off without saying goodbye and slammed the door behind him.

'I'm sorry, love. I don't think he'll ever change his mind. But you'll come and see us again, won't you? Come for my sake at least.'

'I'll see, Mum. Maybe you could come and see us? I'm sure Nellie wouldn't mind. She's a lovely lady.'

'Perhaps. We'll have to see how things work out. Now, why don't you go and sort out your things. You said you wanted to take some stuff back with you. I'll make the tea while you do that.'

'I can at least help you wash the pots before I go. I wasn't planning to leave till later anyway. If Dad's working for the afternoon, we can chat a bit more.'

'I don't want him to come in for his tea and be horrible to you any more.'

'It's all right. I'll get away before then.'

She went up to her old room. It looked just the same as always. There were clean sheets on the bed, ready for her to come back if she chose. Her clothes hung in the wardrobe, all clean and pressed.

Her mother must have grieved a bit when she'd done all that or maybe it had been done with a degree of hope. She took out one or two of her favourite dresses and some jumpers. Her mother came in with some string and brown paper to make a parcel.

'I should have brought my bag back with me, shouldn't I?' Daisy said. 'I didn't really think.' She made a neat parcel of her things and they went down together. 'I'm sorry, Mum, but you do understand, don't you? I'd come back like a shot if Joe could come too. He says he'd never been happier than when he was working here. He loves the animals and working the land. He even wanted Nellie to buy some chickens and a cow so he could make a little farm in her city garden.'

Mrs Baines laughed and gave her daughter a hug.

'Oh, love, you've done me a power of good coming over like this. Let's have our tea and wash the pots and then I'll walk you down the lane to get the bus.'

The yard was quiet.

'Where is everybody?' Daisy asked.

'I expect Terry's gone out in field with the cows. It's almost time he was bringing them up for milking. Your dad was going to plough the bottom field, I think. That's what he said at breakfast time.'

'But the tractor's still at the back of the barn. I can just see it,' Daisy said.

'That's odd. I'd better see if everything's all right.' She pushed open the gate and Daisy followed, still clutching her parcel of clothes. 'Oh my dear lord! Your dad's lying down beside the tractor. He must have fallen.'

They both rushed over to him and called out. They were answered with a loud groan. 'Tom? What's happened?' Mrs Baines shouted.

'Bloomin' thing backfired. Starting handle kicked back and knocked me for six. I think my arm's broken and I can't stand. My leg twisted under me when I tried to get up. You'll have to get help.'

'Oh, goodness me. I'll get Terry.'

'It's all right, Mum. We'll get him into the trap and we can and take him to the doctor's. If we can't move him, I'll go round to fetch the doctor. I'll go and catch the pony and get him hitched. Leave Terry to do the milking. You stay with Dad and try to keep him calm.'

'That useless lad can't do the milking on his own. He gets in a terrible mess if I'm not there to help him.'

'Well, Mum can help out or I'll do that and Mum can drive the pony trap. I'll go and harness it up, anyway.'

With great difficulty, they helped the farmer into the back. He groaned at every move and grumbled at everything they were trying to do. In the end, Mrs Baines went to help with the milking while Daisy drove her father to the doctor's. It was over two miles and the man was clearly suffering every jolt of the way.

'I'm afraid the doctor's been called

out,' his wife said. 'He should be back in an hour or so. You'd better come inside and wait, if you manage to get out, that is. Hang on a minute, we've got an old bath chair somewhere. That would help, I'm sure.'

'I don't want no bath chairs,' grumbled Mr Baines but he was ignored and the doctor's wife disappeared round the side of the building. After a few minutes she arrived pushing a rather dusty looking bath chair.

'It's been in the shed for a while, but at least it saves you putting weight on that leg. It may be broken from the look of it.'

It was a terrible job to load him into the bath chair, but at last the two women managed it. The waiting room was at the side of the main house and somehow, they managed to get him inside.

The consulting room had been converted from the old drawing room of the once rather grand house. It was not quite as smart as Cobridge House and considerably smaller but at least it provided a service in this rural community.

'What's all this going to cost?' grumbled her father.

'It costs whatever it costs,' Daisy snapped. 'You clearly need treatment and you can't work without it so just accept it.'

'Show some respect, girl,' he demanded.

'Respect needs to be earned,' she replied, wondering where she had suddenly found the confidence to speak to her father in that tone. He glared at her, but was suddenly overcome with a new wave of pain and leaned back looking pale and even slightly vulnerable. The usually blustering man was subdued and needed help.

After what seemed an age, the doctor returned and came through the waiting room.

'Good afternoon. Looks as if you've been in the wars. I'll take you through and you can tell me what's been happening.'

Daisy sat in the waiting room,

looking at the old magazines that lay on the table. She could hear the murmur of voices from next door, but not what was being said.

She wondered what the time was and whether she would be able to get her father back before it got dark. And what about her bus back? She had a nasty feeling she was going to miss the last bus and would have to stay at the farm overnight. She might even have to stay on for a few days to help them if her father was going to be unable to work for a while.

She would have to let Joe know or he'd be worried, but there was nothing she could about it at present. At last the surgery door opened and her father was led out.

'I've strapped his arm and splinted his leg. He mustn't put weight on it for a few days. I suspect it's badly sprained, but I'm fairly certain his arm is broken. I've done what I can and he'll need to keep it in the sling. He'll have to use a walking stick as he hasn't got two arms available for crutches.'

The doctor was sounding quite matter of fact and seemed not to understand the implications of his words. How could a farmer not have the use of neither arm or leg?

'Goodness. This complicates matters. I don't know what on earth we shall do. I don't see how I can even get him home in the pony trap.' Daisy had gone quite pale and felt almost panicky.

'If you like, I could drive him back in my car. If you can manage the trap on your own.'

'Well, yes, I suppose so. Thank you. It would be quicker for him and probably more comfortable.'

'How much is it going to cost?' Mr Baines asked again.

'I'll send you the bill later. My wife sorts out the accounts. But I'll drive you back anyway. As a kindness.'

'Well, that's all right, then. Very civil of you. Thank you.'

'Yes, thank you very much,' Daisy added. 'If you'll excuse me, I'd better get on my way or it will be dark before I get back.'

She drove along the road carefully, slightly afraid the pony would become skittish in the dark. Shadows and night-time animals moving around could often frighten a pony when he was unused to night journeys.

The doctor passed her in his car when she was a short way into her journey. By the time she reached their lane, it was almost pitch dark and she was most relieved to reach the farm. She took the trap into the stable and unhitched the pony. She turned him loose into the field and fed him a bucket of oats, patting his hot flanks.

'Good boy. You got me home safely.' She left him and went into the house.

'Hello, love. My, I'm relieved to see you home safely. That wasn't very nice for you, was it?'

'Not really. But I'm OK. I've put the pony out and given him some feed. I'm afraid I've missed my bus back.'

'Your room is always ready for you,

love, and I've got some supper on. Your dad's going to sleep on the couch. There's no way he can go upstairs for a bit. I don't know how we're going to manage.'

'There is a simple way. Joe can come back and help out. I can stay as well and do the dairy work again. Terry and Joe will manage the farm between them.'

'But Terry's got Joe's old room. Where's Joe going to sleep?'

'If Dad's stopping downstairs, I can move in with you and he can have my room for now. Once Dad's better, Terry can go and we can get back to normal.'

'I don't know how your dad'll take it.'

'As the best thing all round. It's the only solution. He'll just have to put up with it. I'll telephone Nellie's house tomorrow morning and explain what's happened.'

They were all exhausted after the strange day and decided to go to bed early. The two women would probably have to take on the milking the following day so it would be an early start. Daisy settled in her own room, thinking how strange it felt to be back there, even after so short a time.

A Return

Joe had been to the bus stop several times to meet at least three different buses, but Daisy had not appeared. He went back to Nellie's where supper was waiting.

'I don't know what's happened to her,' he said anxiously to his sister.

'Maybe she missed the bus and is staying over.'

'No, she wouldn't do that. She was positive she'd be back this evening. She promised.'

'Perhaps something's happened and she's had to stay.'

'Are you sure she hasn't used that telephone contraption of yours?'

'I've told you, no she hasn't. It hasn't rung all day.'

'Something's wrong. I know it is.'

'Let's have our supper, at least. We can save her some if she comes in later.

Come on. Knowing you, you must be starving.'

'I'm worried, our Nellie. S'pose they've kept her there. Her dad's that against me he might have locked her in her room.'

'Oh, for goodness sake, Joe. This is nineteen-thirty-one, not the fifteenth century. Now come on. Let's eat. I'm hungry myself.'

They went into the breakfast room for supper, feeling it was less formal. Joe managed to eat three chops, despite claiming a lack of appetite. He also put away a sizeable portion of apple pie without too much of a problem.

'When do you think James will get home?' he asked.

'Not until late. He was having a meeting and then they were going out to dinner. I doubt he'll be back much before midnight.'

'Right. Well, I don't think I'll wait any longer. Thanks for feeding me. I'll get on my way.'

'What are you planning, Joe?' Nellie

asked suspiciously.

'Nothing. I'll see you tomorrow. Night.'

He left the house and almost ran down the street. Nellie watched him from the window. She knew he was up to something, but there was nothing much she could do about it. It would all have to happen when James was out.

Convinced Daisy was in some sort to trouble, Joe had made up his mind that he needed to go to the farm and find out what was going on. James and his car were out of the question and the last bus had gone so there was only one thing for it.

He would have to walk the eight miles or so. It was quite dark and mostly country lanes once he'd left the outskirts of the town. There was never much traffic around so a lift was also unlikely and the last bus had gone hours ago. He tried to keep his spirits up by whistling but as he got more and more tired, he saved his breath for walking. He'd been working in the garden all day so was feeling quite exhausted.

'I'm coming, Daisy,' he whispered. He couldn't bear to think of anything hurting his girl. He'd kill that father of hers if he'd done anything to harm her.

He didn't recognise where he was in the dark and hoped it wasn't too much further. It must be nearly midnight by now, he thought . . . and there must still be a long way to go.

After Joe left, Nellie paced up and down the room. She felt totally unsettled and finally decided to go and see her parents. It wasn't far and she had to know Joe had gone straight home.

He'd been so worried, she suspected he might try to go after Daisy. She told Mrs Potts where she was going, in case James arrived home and wondered where she was.

'Shall I get someone to walk with you, ma'am?' she asked kindly. 'Only I doubt the master would take too kindly you wandering the streets on your own this late at night.'

'It's not far. My brother will walk me back. Or my father. I'll be fine.'

'Hello, love. What are you doing here? Is Joe with you?' Nan asked, surprised to see her oldest daughter so late at night.

'Hasn't he come home?' Nan shook her head. 'I bet he's gone off to find Daisy.'

Quickly she explained what had happened and decided to go home again, in case James arrived home earlier than expected. 'I think he's walking to the Baines farm. Silly boy. He might lose his way in the dark. I'll see if James will drive out there if he gets back in time. Don't worry, Mum. I'm sure he'll be fine.'

'Wait on, I'll get our Ben to walk you back home. He's been wanting to have a talk to you anyway.'

Nellie and her younger brother set off back to her house.

'Haven't seen anything of you for ages,' she said to him.

'Been busy. I've been doing some drawings and stuff and I wanted to show them to you. Mum said as you might be able to help me with a job. I don't want to stay on at school for ever. I'm sick of it and I'm not doing anything I want to be doing.'

'You're a bit young to think of leaving. You're only fifteen.'

'But I could go to that college you talked about. Learn about potting, proper like. And work at the factory in between. What do you say?'

'I'll need to think about it a little. Just now though, I've got other things on my mind. So, what's happening in your life, apart from being sick of school?'

They chatted as they walked and Nellie realised how far away from her younger siblings she had grown. Perhaps this was the way with all families but still, she felt slightly guilty.

She had once been so close to them all, especially Lizzie. Now the little girl was growing up without her big sister to look after her.

Ben had always been closer to Joe so he must have felt a bit lonely at times. She must somehow find time to change all that and show more interest in what they were doing.

'Life does get complicated at times, doesn't it?' she said.

'Dunno about that. Pretty boring most of the time. Any road, can I bring my drawings round to show you soon?'

'Course you can, love. Come round at the weekend. I'm looking for something new for the next range.'

'Aren't you going to ask me in?' Ben asked.

'Not this evening. Thanks for coming back with me, but you need to get back and go to bed. It's late and anyway, you've got school tomorrow. Night, night.'

'Night, Nellie. Hope you find our Joe.'

She watched him walk back down the road. He was a tall lad, surprisingly sensitive and quite good looking, she realised.

She looked forward to seeing his drawings and hoped that he might really have a talent in designing pottery.

It would be good to have one of her own family working with her. She pushed open the door and Mrs Potts came out of her little sitting room.

'Have there been any phone messages?' she asked.

'No, Ma'am. Nothing. But the Master's back. He's in the drawing room having a nightcap.'

'Thank you, Mrs Potts. Good night.' She went into the drawing room and told James about the strange events of the day. 'I think the stupid lad has walked off to the farm to see what's happened.'

'What? Walking all the way to near Barlaston in the dark? It's eight miles and more.'

'I know, but he was that worried. Seems to think Mr Baines would lock Daisy in and stop her returning. I think he's a bit unbalanced . . . Mr Baines, I mean, of course.'

'So what do you want to do?'

'I wondered if we should drive over there and look for him.'

'He could be anywhere. He might have cut across country and we'd just miss him anyway.'

'Oh dear, why didn't I take up your offer to learn to drive?'

'Hey, don't worry, Nellie. Joe's a strong lad. How long since he left?'

'Must be nearly two hours.'

'He might be almost there, then. Oh, come on then. Better tell someone we're going out again.' He swallowed the last of his drink and went to get his coat.

They drove quickly along the familiar route, assuming Joe would be nearer the farm than anywhere else. There was no sign of him anywhere. At last they arrived at the lane leading to the farm and still without any sight of Joe. The whole place was in darkness.

'What now?' James asked. 'Looks as if they're all in bed. I don't relish waking them up and having old man Baines shouting me off the land.'

'Oh dear, I just don't know. I suppose Joe must have gone across the fields. Or maybe he's lost his bearings in the dark. It's raining now too and I hate to think of him out there getting cold and wet. Shall we drive into the village? Look for him there?'

'If you like.' James gave a loud yawn. 'We'll take a look, but I'm absolutely worn out. I can't drive round all night. Perhaps he's arrived at the farm and gone to sleep in a barn or something.'

'We can't go and look, I suppose?' Nellie suggested.

'Certainly not. The dogs would all start barking and then there's be chaos.'

'OK, then we'd better drive back through the village. Oh dear, he could be anywhere. I'm sorry, James.'

'It's all right, darling. I know how much your family means to you. Stop worrying. He'll be fine.'

'I suppose so.'

They drove slowly, peering into the hedges at the sides of the road and looked into gateways. There was no sign. At last, they decided to give up and go home.

'Not that I'll get any sleep,' Nellie told her husband. 'But you need some sleep so we'd best give up. How was your evening anyway?' she asked finally.

'Very good, actually. I was chatting to another producer and he was telling me they are looking at introducing a new system for firing the pottery. Expensive to install, but it'll save a lot of money in the long run. A continuous belt system. Very up-to-date and it avoids all the tiresome loading of the bottle kilns and waiting for it to cool before unloading. Save a huge amount of manpower.'

'And a lot of jobs.' Nellie was too weary to think of the implications of what her husband was saying with such enthusiasm. 'But please, can we talk about it another time?'

'Just thought you might be interested.'

'It sounds wonderful, but I'm tired, worried and beginning to feel very cold.

Oh dear, if I'm cold sitting in the car, how must Joe be feeling if he's sleeping somewhere out in the open?'

Despite her worries, Nellie fell asleep the moment she got into bed. She was troubled by dreams but didn't awake till after six o'clock the next morning. She dressed quickly and went down to the kitchen. Ethel had got the kettle on and was about to make tea.

'Did you find your brother?' she asked.

'No. I don't know where he went. I'm afraid he got himself lost in the dark. I'll have some tea and then go to see if he went back to my parents' house. After that, I'll just have to wait and see.'

★　★　★

When the rain began and he realised he was lost, Joe looked for shelter. He should have reached the farm lane by now, he thought. How could he have gone wrong on such a simple journey?

He reached a field gate and climbed

over it. Maybe there would be some sort of animal shelter nearby. If he had to share it with some sheep or cows, he wasn't bothered. He needed to sit and rest and get out of the rain. He walked along the inside of the hedge and found a tumbledown shed. It was hardly dry but it offered some shelter. He closed his eyes, meaning to rest for a few moments but fell into a deep sleep.

He awoke stiff and cold some hours later and saw a chink of light appearing through a hole in the roof. At least the rain had stopped and maybe now it was light enough for him to see where he was. He rubbed cold hands together and stood up, stamping his feet to restore the circulation.

A curious herd of cattle came close to inspect him. Young bullocks, he could see they were. He thought they must be Ashton's herd so he was very close to the Baines' farm after all.

'Go on,' he called to the cattle and they skittered away as he waved his arms. He went back to the gate and climbed out of the field. He still failed to recognise the muddy track and retraced his steps back to the lane he had left during the night.

Dawn was beginning to break properly now and he could make out the lines of hedgerows more clearly. He climbed a tall oak at the side of another field to get a better view of where he was. He could just make out some familiar farm buildings and set off again with relief and renewed energy.

He was uncertain what would happen when he finally arrived at the farm, but he had to know what had happened to Daisy.

Wearily he knocked on the door, hoping that it wasn't Mr Baines who opened it.

'Joe, what on earth are you doing here? You look terrible. Come on in.' Unbelievably to Joe, it was Daisy opening the door, looking pretty and quite relaxed.

'Are you all right, Daisy? Only I was worried out of my mind when you didn't come back.'

'I'm fine. Sit yourself by the fire and I'll pour you some tea. Then I'll get some warm food into you.'

They exchanged details of the events of the past day and night and realised what they had to do.

'I'll tell my dad that you're here and can take over his work. Terry can carry on with the milking and Mum and I will do the dairy between us. I'm not sure how it will work out in the end, but at least we can keep things going.'

'Right. But first I'll have to let our Nellie know what's going on. She'll be worried and I bet she'll be pestering Mum to know where I am. I'll go to the village and use that telephone thing.'

'When you've got a decent breakfast inside you.' She busied herself frying bacon and Joe leaned back in what was usually Mr Baines, chair by the fire.

Within seconds he was asleep. Daisy smiled fondly. Lucky her dad was firmly fixed on the sofa in the other room or he'd have complained bitterly. Her mum came into the room and Daisy pointed at Joe, putting her finger to her mouth to tell Mrs Baines to be quiet. She whispered the story to her and suggested she took tea into Mr Baines and brought him up speed with the events.

'At least Joe's here to help out now. Once he's let his sister know we're both safe, he'll set to work. Just like old times again, isn't it?'

'I doubt anything will ever be quite the same again,' Mrs Baines said wryly. 'I'll take his tea in.'

* * *

Nellie was very relieved to know that Joe was safe.

'So what does Mr Baines think of it all? Is he going to let you stay?'

'He doesn't have a choice in the matter. He's helpless and if I don't stay, the farm's as good as over and done with.'

'Well take care, love, and keep in touch. It's very generous of you to offer to help under the circumstances. I'm proud of you, Joe.'

'Thanks, our Nellie. These telephone things are pretty good, aren't they? Tell Mum I'm all right.' He put the receiver down and went back to the farm, his step lighter despite his weariness from the night.

He was back with his beloved animals and close to his girl. As long as Mr Baines stayed firmly on the sofa, he felt free to run things as he wanted. That Terry had better knuckle down to working properly or he'd have some-thing to say. You couldn't mess about with the herd and still get proper results.

The next few days were among the happiest he could remember. Mr Baines could be heard grumbling away in the other room, but he could scarcely move so Joe left him to it. He took over the milking, not willing to rely on Terry's slapdash ways. He made the lad scrape the yard and do a lot of the less pleasant jobs around the place. He worked him much harder than the farmer had done and after a couple more days, he suddenly announced he'd had enough.

'Can't stick this place any more. I'm going home. Give me what's owed and I'm off.'

'But you can't go while we need you,' protested Mrs Baines. 'My husband's going to be laid low for a while yet.'

'It's all right, Mrs Baines. I can manage by myself. With a bit of help from Daisy sometimes. Besides, I'll be glad to have my old room back. Daisy's room is very nice, but it's a bit pink.'

Trying to keep a straight face, Mrs Baines took out the cash box and paid Terry his few coins that were owed. He nodded and stuffed them in his pocket. With a very small bundle of clothes, he went off down the lane.

'Good riddance,' muttered Daisy. 'What a very unpleasant lad he is. But we shall have our work cut out to manage everything properly.'

'No problem,' Joe said. 'I've worked

out how we can manage. As long as Mrs Baines is willing to do the cooking and some of the dairy work, you can help with feeding the stock and cleaning the milking parlour. If you're willing, of course.'

'Is that all right with you, Mum? It should please Dad no end saving another whole lot of wages.'

'It sounds grand. You're a kind lad, Joe. Our Daisy couldn't have done any better, I reckon.'

'Thanks Mrs B. Just hope her father comes round to thinking the same, one day,' Joe replied.

Peace At Last

Life at Cobridge House seemed to have settled back into a more comfortable routine. James still remained worried about work related matters, but for Nellie it seemed that her worries and doubts about her future were subsiding.

Mrs Potts was proving to be a perfect choice of housekeeper. She was firm with the girls but not as unapproachable as Mrs Wilkinson had been. They all seemed to like her and the new young maid was proving willing and eager to learn. She was not unlike the younger Nellie had once been when she first arrived.

'Do you think we can manage another dinner party?' James asked. 'There are a couple of the other manufacturers I'd like to ask round. It's this business of the dust. There's an agreement in the melting pot and I want the chance to discuss it informally. Away from work.'

Nellie's heart sank. She hated these affairs at the best of times but as James always put up with her own family whenever she asked him to, she could hardly refuse something as important as business dinners. She rang the bell and asked Mrs Potts to come and see her. The worthy woman was not fazed in any way and made notes on exact requirements for the dinner.

★　★　★

'What do you think of these, Vera?' Nellie asked her colleague at the factory.

'Interesting. Don't look quite like your style. But they are good. Bit different from the stuff we've been doing lately, but films and cinema are getting more and more popular. So, are you going to tell me where these designs came from?'

'My brother, Ben. He's been working

away for ages and brought them round to show me. I said I'd think about it. He wants to come to join us here and go to the college to study.'

'I think he's got some talent. Maybe they'll come in one day. I liked your bright coffee sets, by the way, but aren't they expensive?'

The sample sets Nellie had commissioned had turned out well. James and his sales team had also loved them, but they were certainly at the luxury end of the market with their solid gold painted insides.

'They are a bit. I need to do a coffee pot and sugar and cream to go with them. Easy enough. We have some stock shapes we can use.'

Excited by her new idea. Nellie went along to the company's small library. There were always a collection of magazines and a number of art books on the shelves.

She found pictures by some of the French impressionists and was thrilled to think of ways she could incorporate them into her china. She carried a heap of them back to her office and she worked steadily for the rest of the day, lost in a world she had been missing for a long time. It was almost six o'clock when James knocked on her door.

'I was wondering where you'd disappeared to. Are you ready to go home? What are you doing?'

'Some new ideas. I'm quite excited. It's something entirely different to our usual stuff.'

James picked up Ben's designs and scanned them.

'This is certainly different. Is this what's got you so involved?'

'Oh, no. That's Ben's stuff. It's quirky, isn't it?'

'Certainly unusual. He's probably got some raw talent here. Must take after his sister. Are you going to take him on?'

'I think so. Not sure quite how to work it yet, but he's so enthusiastic, I'd like to help him.'

'Give him an apprenticeship. Let him

work his way through the factory. No favours, though, and he'll have to know his place. No popping up to see you when things go wrong.'

'Thanks, James. I think that would be perfect. You know something? Life is looking good. I've had a great day. Just like old times.'

'Can I remind you that you have a small son at home who will be waiting to see you before he goes to bed.'

'Oh, poor William. After all my claims that I was going to spend time with him. I'm not such a good mother after all. I wonder how Joe and Daisy are getting on?'

'Nellie Cobridge. You're impossible. You have a mind like a grasshopper. Once one thing is sorted you're off worrying about something else. You haven't mentioned Lizzie for the last five minutes. Aren't you worried something needs to be done for her?'

'Well, now you mention it, I was just . . .'

'Nellie,' he shouted. 'Stop it right

now. Give me a kiss.'

'What? Here?'

'If it's the only way to shut you up, yes. Right here.' She did as he was told. 'Welcome back, darling girl,' James said happily.

★ ★ ★

Joe had been working the farm for almost two weeks. He was feeling weary most evenings but very satisfied that he was managing well. Daisy was working hard too but enjoying being with him for much of every day.

Mr Baines had almost given up asking for daily reports on what was happening. Joe had kept right out of his way and sent Mrs Baines in to pass on the news. He was always anxious to know if milk production was falling and if the quality was up to standard.

'You sure those two youngsters are behaving?' he asked his wife at least twice every day.

'Oh, Tom, of course they are. They're

both working so hard they are exhausted. They're very sweet.'

He lay back, bored out of his mind and desperate to get back to normal. He tried flexing his hand and found that there was a bit more movement lately. It still gave him pain and he still couldn't walk for more than a few yards.

Still, if his wife was right, the farm wasn't going under. Joe must be working hard to manage everything. Perhaps he wasn't such a bad lad after all.

'Maybe I've been a bit hasty. We should let them get betrothed,' Mr Baines eventually said to his wife after much reflection.

'Oh, Tom, thank you. They'll be thrilled.'

'I didn't say as they could get wed. Just betrothed.'

'It's a good start. Shall I tell them or will you?'

'I thought I might try to come and eat supper at the table tonight. I can move about a bit more now. We could tell them then.'

'That's wonderful. I'll try to keep it a

'secret till then, but it'll be hard.'

'For heaven's sake, woman. You're as daft as those two.' But he had a smile on his own face when she had gone. He'd had too much time to think lately.

His enforced rest had made him realise he was getting on a bit and needed to make sure his farm was going to be properly looked after.

She could look after him and Mrs Baines when they were really old. And, he'd be able to keep an eye on everything, make sure things were being done as he wanted them to be.

'Is someone coming to supper?' Daisy asked when she came in and saw the extra place set at the table.

'Your dad's feeling better and wants to eat with us,' Mrs Baines told her.

'Well I hope he's not going to start on us if he's feeling better. We're doing really well without him interfering.'

'Oh, I don't think you'll be worried. You might even be pleased.'

'Mum? Why are you smiling like that?'

'No reason. I'm pleased he's making an effort again. I've been worried about him. He's never had to sit still for so long in his life.'

'At least he's got all the book-work up to date,' Daisy smiled. 'Must be a first. Anyway, what's for supper? I'm starving and so's Joe.'

By the time Joe had come in and washed, Mr Baines was already seated at the table. He looked pale and wearied by his efforts. Joe hoped there wasn't going to be any trouble. He'd been enjoying the relaxed atmosphere that had existed lately.

They ate the delicious stew and vegetables in almost total silence. Nobody seemed willing to start any conversation. When the plates were removed, Mr Baines cleared his throat.

'I've got something to say,' he began. Joe and Daisy exchanged worried glances. 'I've been impressed with the way you two have knuckled down to working since I've been laid up. Your mother says there's been nothing unpleasant going on so I'm saying that I'm willing for you to get betrothed. You're still too young to get wed, but we can agree to an arrangement between you.'

'Oh Dad, that's great!' Daisy exclaimed. 'Thanks. Oh, Joe, at least that means you can stay here for good.'

'Thanks, Mr Baines. I'm glad you've come round. Can I ask what age you think we shall be old enough to get wed properly?'

Mrs Baines looked anxious.

'Don't worry, Joe, love. It needn't be for too long. Be happy that this grumpy old man of mine has at least agreed to something.'

Daisy looked at her father, wondering how he'd take that comment, but he still seemed to be smiling.

'Well, you'd have to be at least eighteen, the age me and your mother got wed.'

'But I'm going to be eighteen in two days time.'

'So you are, girl.'

'Does that mean . . . ?' Joe held his breath.

'Well, you can't get wed on Friday, you daft pair. Oh, for goodness' sake. Once I'm up and about again, we'll think about it then. Now Mother, haven't you got that ring of your grandmother's stuck away somewhere? Our Daisy could have that for her eighteenth birthday and it will serve as an engagement ring as well. Save buying her another present as well.'

'She can certainly have Granny's ring but it isn't her only present. Besides, Joe might want to get her a ring himself.'

'I don't need any rings or anything else. Just my Joe to be mine forever.'

'Oh shut up, can't you. I don't like hearing all this soppy talk. Clear off out, the pair of you. Go for a walk or something and give me some peace. Lovey-dovey nonsense. 'Tain't natural.'

'That's just what it is, love,' Mrs Baines laughed. 'Come here, you two. I can't tell you how pleased I am. Now, why don't you go down to the village and use that telephone to call your sister? I reckon as she deserves to hear the good news. We must see about getting a telephone put in here. Save an awful lot of walking out.'

'And just how much do you think that would cost?' roared Mr Baines.

'Probably just about what you've saved with Joe and our Daisy working so hard these past weeks.'

Hand in hand, the pair almost ran down the lane, laughing with delight.

Epilogue

Early the next spring, plans for the wedding were complete. It had been decided that the reception should take place at Cobridge House. Though Mrs Baines would have liked to have it at the farm, practicality took over.

Nellie's staff would do all the preparation and there was plenty of room for everyone to enjoy the feast. For Nellie herself, it was the sort of occasion she had missed at the time of her own marriage.

They had married in secret with neither reception nor honeymoon, save a few stolen days some time later. She fussed around making everything as perfect as possible.

'Don't go too far over the top,' James advised. 'We don't want people to feel uncomfortable because it's all too much for them to cope with.'

'Oh, dear. Am I making it too posh?'

'You are a bit. I don't want to sound snobbish, but they do live in the country and from what Joe says, they are used to a simple life.'

'Oh, dear. What shall I do? I just want everything to be perfect for them.'

'Just relax. Let your mother come round and see what's being arranged. She's a sensible lady. She'll soon put you right.'

'Thanks, James. Good advice. You're a wonderful man and I'm lucky you managed to put up with me all this time.'

'It seems as if everything has come right in the end, doesn't it? The problems in the pottery industry are resolved for the time being. Your latest designs look like doing really well.

'Ben seems to have settled well at the factory and now Joe and Daisy have their future sorted. William's turning into a well-behaved little boy and a constant joy. In fact, I was thinking, isn't it about time he had a little brother or sister?'

'Oh, for goodness' sake, James. When would I ever have time to bring up another baby?'

'I was thinking how much your family mean to you. Isn't it a shame that he won't have any siblings?'

'You managed on your own.'

'Did I, though? Look how much I've changed since I got to know you and your family. A large and loving family seems to me to be one of the most important things in life. Please think about it.'

'I will,' she promised. 'But now, I've got to think about two hundred other details. I need to see Mrs Potts right away. I'm not sure if she's ordered enough flowers for the tables.'

'Oh, Nellie, you'll never change will you? Promise me you won't, anyway!'

★ ★ ★

The wedding day arrived at last. Joe had spent the previous night with his parents and, much to Nan's disgust, the men had been down to the miner's club and had more beer than she thought reasonable.

They came round to Cobridge House at ten o'clock slightly the worse for wear. Nellie was suitably cross with them and spent a few minutes trying to pull neckties straight and pinning carnations into buttonholes. Lizzie looked as pretty as a picture in a lemon bridesmaid's dress with a wreath of primroses on her head.

The redoubtable Mrs Potts had made it herself with fresh flowers from the garden, yet another of her endless talents. Lizzie was to commence her bridesmaid's duties when they met at the church as it had been decided it would be more practical than being driven out to the farm.

Impatient to be there when the bride arrived, Lizzie and her family set out early. Nervously, Joe waited inside the church with James by his side, as best man.

The groom gasped as he saw Daisy walking towards him, pretty as a picture in her lace dress, the same one worn by her mother for her own wedding. After all their difficulties, the day had finally arrived. He was surrounded by the people he loved most and about to start on his life's journey.

'Don't they make a lovely couple?' Nellie whispered to her mother.

'I'm so proud of my family,' Nan said, tears streaming down her cheeks. 'Who'd have thought a poor miner and his wife could have produced such a wonderful collection of people?'

'You're right, Mum. And I know now that I must do something about making us a bit more of a family of our own.'